"I Never Thought I'd See The Day When I'd Be Entertaining Travis Banks In My Bedroom," Lauren Said.

"Why not?"

"Need I remind you that when you were a senior in high school, you couldn't be bothered to give a little nobody freshman like me the time of day?"

Travis looked as if he were taxing his memory. "I don't recall you ever asking me for it."

"I didn't have the nerve," Lauren admitted.

"Actually, I do vaguely recall you just about melting into the floor the few times I tried to make eye contact with you."

"I'm afraid you still have the same effect on me," she confessed.

"You have a different effect on me now."

Travis's voice was laden with palpable implications. Lauren could not have dreamed a more delicious scene than the one that was unfolding right now.

Now was not the time for caution.

Dear Reader,

This May, Silhouette Desire's sensational lineup starts with Nalini Singh's *Awaken the Senses*. This DYNASTIES: THE ASHTONS title is a tale of sexual awakening starring one seductive Frenchman. (Can you say ooh-la-la?) Also for your enjoyment this month is the launch of Maureen Child's trilogy. The THREE-WAY WAGER series focuses on the Reilly brothers, triplets who bet each other they can stay celibate for ninety days. But wait until brother number one is reunited with *The Tempting Mrs. Reilly*.

Susan Crosby's BEHIND CLOSED DOORS series continues with *Heart of the Raven,* a gothic-toned story of a man whose self-imposed seclusion has cut him off from love…until a sultry woman, and a beautiful baby, open up his heart. Brenda Jackson is back this month with a new Westmoreland story, in *Jared's Counterfeit Fiancée,* the tale of a fake engagement that leads to real passion. Don't miss Cathleen Galitz's *Only Skin Deep,* a delightful transformation story in which a shy girl finally falls into bed with the man she's always dreamed about. And rounding out the month is *Bedroom Secrets* by Michelle Celmer, featuring a hero to die for.

Thanks for choosing Silhouette Desire, where we strive to bring you the best in smart, sensual romances. And in the months to come look for a new installment of our TEXAS CATTLEMAN'S CLUB continuity and a brand-new TANNERS OF TEXAS title from the incomparable Peggy Moreland.

Happy reading!

Melissa Jeglinski

Melissa Jeglinski
Senior Editor
Silhouette Books

Please address questions and book requests to:
Silhouette Reader Service
U.S.: 3010 Walden Ave., P.O. Box 1325, Buffalo, NY 14269
Canadian: P.O. Box 609, Fort Erie, Ont. L2A 5X3

ONLY SKIN DEEP

CATHLEEN GALITZ

Silhouette®

Desire

Published by Silhouette Books

America's Publisher of Contemporary Romance

SILHOUETTE BOOKS

ISBN 0-373-76655-6

ONLY SKIN DEEP

Copyright © 2005 by Cathleen Galitz

Books by Cathleen Galitz

Silhouette Desire

The Cowboy Takes a Bride #1271
Wyoming Cinderella #1373
Her Boss's Baby #1396
Tall, Dark...and Framed? #1433
Warrior in Her Bed #1506
Pretending with the Playboy #1569
Cowboy Crescendo #1591
Only Skin Deep #1655

Silhouette Romance

The Cowboy Who Broke the Mold #1257
100% Pure Cowboy #1279
Wyoming Born & Bred #1381

CATHLEEN GALITZ,

a Wyoming native, teaches English to students in grades six to twelve in a rural school that houses kindergartners and seniors in the same building. She feels blessed to have married a man who is both supportive and patient. When she's not busy writing, teaching or chauffeuring her sons to and from various activities, she can most likely be found indulging in her favorite pastime—reading.

To Amber who has always been there
for me no matter what.

One

Lauren Hewett felt an eerie connection to the imaginary person playing the piano in the corner of the room. Like him, she too was invisible. Actually, the ghost pianist had the advantage over her. He could at least make himself heard, if not seen—something Lauren hadn't been able to manage since shortly after her thirty-fifth birthday. She wasn't sure exactly what caused this phenomenon, only that one day she woke up and found herself of an age when no one bothered to ask her opinion on matters of importance anymore, or treat her as anything other than an oddity.

As the background music ground to a halt, she gave the antique player piano another crank and reached inside herself for a smile. Smiling vacuously was, after all, one of a maid of honor's many duties—especially when she was the daughter of the bride. Still, Lauren couldn't help but heave a little sigh of regret when a figure clad in ivory lace made her way up the gleaming spiral staircase in the foyer. The bride was the focal point of a room tastefully bedecked with the very floral combination Lauren always envisioned for her own wedding: pink roses, miniature white carnations and baby's breath.

"Always the bridesmaid, never the bride," she muttered under her breath.

Fighting back a wave of melancholy, Lauren focused her attention on a montage of framed pictures hanging on the wall behind her. In her favorite, a little girl with wide green eyes and dark pigtails sat upon her father's lap, blissfully unaware that he would pass out of this world before his only daughter would receive her high school diploma. The woman standing behind the two of them with a hand lovingly draped on her husband's shoulder was a younger version of the smiling bride who was at the moment addressing her guests from halfway up the stairs.

Lauren touched a finger to her own lips before placing it to her father's as if to prevent him from saying anything to ruin the moment.

"Don't worry, Daddy. You'd like him. He makes Mom happy."

Across the crowded room, she caught a glimpse of Travis Banks, looking just as bored as she felt. At six-three he stood a good head taller than anyone else in the room. In a tailored black Western suit, he looked even better than she remembered—a feat she hardly thought possible. Lauren was surprised to see him in attendance. It was widely believed that the county's most eligible bachelor avoided all weddings for fear of contracting a highly contagious disease that he was fond of comparing to the plague: *nuptialitis.*

"Hurry up, everybody," a voice called out. "Barbara's about to toss the bouquet."

Younger, prettier and far more visible bachelorettes pressed to the front of the crowd for a chance to catch the flowers that by tradition signaled the end of their single status. Too old and jaded for such nonsense, Lauren faded even more deliberately into the wallpaper and continued to covertly study the man she'd had a crush on since high school. She had been a lowly freshman when, as the senior quarterback for the Wranglers, Travis carried her heart—along with every other girl's in good old Pinedale High over the goal line.

Not that he'd been able to see her back then either....

Lauren decided that time had only improved Travis's boyish good looks. There was no sign of gray in his sandy blond hair, and the weight he'd put on looked to be mostly muscle. Although Lauren had little interest in catching a bouquet, she secretly fantasized about catching *him.* Unfortunately, she doubted she'd be lucky enough to claim a single dance with him all evening.

Certainly not when I look like a cupcake whose frosting runneth over in this hideous pastel gown, she thought to herself. *How can it be possible that my own mother can be married twice when I've yet to so much as be engaged? And all these years I thought I was the one doing Mom a favor by being there for her. Turns out that I'm the one who's been holding her back....*

Determinedly Lauren steered her thoughts away from self-pity to more practical matters. Like where she was going to live now that Cupid's heat-seeking missile had found the target painted on the roof of her house. Not that her mother was kicking her out or anything so melodramatic. It went without saying that she was always welcome here. But while it was one thing to rationalize living at home when she had the excuse of taking care of an aging mother, it was quite another sharing a home with a pair of honeymooners. That they were in their sixties was inconsequential to the fact that Lauren's mother was getting more action than she was...

"Catch, honey!"

Lauren spun around at the sound of her mother's voice. She barely had time to shield her face from a projectile hurtling across the room at her. Barbara Aberdeen should have played high school football herself for all the precision and accuracy of her throw. The crowd cheered—and laughed—as a red-faced Lauren displayed her ill-gotten prize: one bridal bouquet compliments of a well-meaning, if not openly desperate, mother.

Later at the punch bowl, Lauren overheard a disappointed and tipsy Sylvia Porter describe the event as "A pity pass if I ever saw one."

Lauren wouldn't have thought such a petty remark would have the power to sting at her age. But it did.

Maybe even more today than years ago when she and her girlfriends had labored under the misconception that popularity really mattered and dating the right guy was a one-way ticket to happily ever after. The raw wistfulness in Sylvia's voice kept Lauren from confronting the nasty little witch who was so obviously distraught at the thought of ending up as ancient and alone as the day's maid of honor.

Lauren took a deep breath and did her best to let it go. She certainly hadn't made a conscious decision to live her life as the object of anyone's pity. In fact, it wasn't all that long ago she had imagined a life for herself that included a husband and children and the simple joys that so many of her own friends took for granted. As much as they assured her that she was the smart one, unfettered by an endless procession of soccer games and the astronomical price of fixing their children's crooked teeth and having to clean up after chronically lazy husbands, Lauren suspected they were simply being kind. Somewhere between college and tenure in the local public school system, she had turned into the Old Maid in the card game that she so enjoyed playing as a child. If there was any way to reshuffle the deck now without somehow discarding herself in the process, she had yet to find it.

In retrospect, Lauren supposed she'd been too picky back in the days when she'd occasionally accepted a date. The few college guys she'd gone with had been too aggressive for her introverted nature. And after a couple of years of horrible blind dates arranged by well-meaning friends immediately following college, she'd gradually slipped into a routine of work and home and civic duties that distracted her from the fact that everyone else her age was either married—or remarried. Periodically Lauren updated her surroundings with new curtains and bedding so that the passing of years became as familiar to the room in which she'd been sleeping since childhood as the seasons routinely changing outside her window.

Had it not been for her mother's recent revelation that she had fallen in love again and was actually considering Henry Aberdeen's proposal of marriage, Lauren supposed she never would have been forced out of her comfy little rut. Above all, she wanted her mother to be happy. So she had put aside her own personal struggle about betraying her father's memory and encouraged Barbara to follow her heart. After all, if someone as wonderful as her mom was lucky enough to find true love twice in one lifetime, who was her spinster daughter to stand in the way?

That wasn't to say that Lauren wasn't struggling internally with this latest turn of events in her life. If catching the bouquet at your mother's wedding didn't qualify as a defining moment in one's life, she didn't know what did.

Since she doubted there were any books written on reverse empty nests, Lauren poured herself another glass of champagne-laced punch and reconsidered her all too boring life. She wanted to be completely moved out of her mother's house by the time the newlyweds returned from their Caribbean cruise honeymoon. Then she was going to actively start looking for Mr. Right.

Or even Mr. Close Enough.

The fact that decent rentals in the area were about as easy to find as eligible bachelors under the age of six-ty-five was just one obstacle for Lauren to overcome. Another more formidable hurdle was her own innate tentativeness when it came to matters of the heart. She didn't need a therapist to tell her that her fear of intima-cy was rooted in the unexpected heart attack that killed her father when she most needed him. What she really needed was the nerve to overcome her insecurity—and a chance to revive her expired dreams.

As luck would have it, opportunity presented itself in the form of Fenton Marsh who worked up the cour-age behind a pair of pop bottle lenses to sidle up next to her and ask her to dance. Lauren ignored her first in-clination to dismiss him. He was, after all, no Travis Banks. But then again, a girl had to start somewhere, and being standoffish hadn't gotten her anywhere but miserable so far as she could tell.

"I'd be delighted," Lauren heard herself say a little too brightly. She feared that all she was missing was the Southern drawl to make her feel as pathetic as poor Blanche DuBois from *A Streetcar Named Desire.*

Blessedly, her third glass of punch was doing what it was supposed to do: deaden her inhibitions. Heck, if her mother could overlook the groom's balding pate and obsequious pandering for her affection, the least Lauren could do was close her eyes to Fenton's obvious shortcomings and focus on his strengths—something he was more than happy to point out the instant they reached the dance floor.

"I'm guessing you already know that since we went to school together, I've become quite wealthy," he said, crunching on her instep.

Lauren winced. She supposed the fact that his father had left him the only grocery store in town might have something to do with that, but instead she simply murmured how wonderful that must be for him.

Apparently giddy with the impression he was making, Fenton twirled her around like a multicolored chiffon top. Lauren hadn't been expecting the move and consequently caught a heel in the hem of her floor-length gown. Flinging an arm out to steady herself, she connected with a mountain of a man who was doing his best to get his big fingers through the handle of a crystal punch glass. Liquid rained down upon them both.

As Fenton hurried off to get a wet rag, Travis Banks studied the red stain spreading down the front of his expensive white shirt. Looking like a victim of a drive-by shooting, he mumbled, "I'm sorry."

Lauren was perturbed. After all, apologizing for something that wasn't her fault was *her* specialty.

"What for? Being in the wrong place at the wrong time?" she asked, drawing her gaze away from his muscled chest up to his bemused, twinkling gray eyes.

That they reminded her of fog lifting from the top of the Tetons didn't help matters any. That they belonged to the most sought after—and elusive—bachelor in the county didn't do a thing to put her at ease, either.

"For getting in Fred and Ginger's way when they were in the middle of one of their crowd-stopping moves I suppose."

The fact that his country drawl was thick enough to draw flies only served to underscore his charm. Although the music had stopped, Lauren remained frozen in place by a flash of Travis's white teeth. Only when Fred Astair, aka Fenton, returned with a handful of dripping wet paper towels did Lauren realize her own hands were planted squarely on a rock-hard set of pectoral muscles. She drew back as if she were touching a wall of flame instead of all too human flesh.

How tempting it was to peek beneath that tailor-made jacket to see if there wasn't something fake hidden beneath its folds.

Like a heart.

Even sheltered English teachers such as Lauren were privy to the local gossip about how Casanova had nothing on the infamous Travis Banks. How repeated attempts failed to convince him that not all women were like the ex-wife who reputedly had "ruined" him for married life forever. And how he was attempting to pay back the rest of the female race by using up lovers like so many tissues in a box. Not that such bad behavior on his part weakened his standing as the most "ooh-able" match in these sleepy parts. Even married women openly sighed over him.

Often in front of their husbands.

Fenton's return to the scene of the crime had been

swift, however, his fumbling attempts to dab at the punch on Lauren's dress only made matters worse. Blushing to think that she looked like a nursing mother leaking through the bodice of her dress, Lauren blinked back tears. Not a woman given to hysterics, she felt herself precariously close to a public meltdown guaranteed to ruin her mother's special day.

"Anything I can do to help, Lauren?"

Realizing that Travis remembered her name was flattering in itself. Years ago, she'd assumed this golden Adonis had been too busy leading the league in touchdowns and flirting with cheerleaders to notice yet another adoring underclassman in the stands. Since high school, she wasn't sure they even qualified as passing acquaintances. Dismissing the warning bells sounding inside her head, Lauren managed a wobbly smile.

"You could be kind enough to dance with me until I dry off and get myself pulled back together."

It was a presumptuous request, but all of a sudden the very prim and proper Ms. Hewett didn't give a fig about propriety and what others might think. Perhaps it was just wishful thinking to pretend the reason her friends had never tried fixing her up with Travis was because of his well-known aversion to marriage. Perhaps knowing his reputation as a heartbreaker, they wanted to protect her. It was more likely that they thought that he was out of her league. Nevertheless, having just committed herself to meeting as many potential suitors as possible, she saw nothing wrong with starting with the best-looking one first.

Besides, being seen with the most notorious bachelor in the county could only promote the fact that Lauren Hewett was putting herself back on the market.

The last thing Travis Banks wanted to do was dance with the woman who had just ruined his best shirt. He'd planned on making an appearance and hanging around only long enough to toast the wedding couple before making a quick getaway. Weddings in general made him uneasy. At the present he was surrounded by so many female biological clocks ticking in synch that they almost drowned out the band.

Not that bookish Lauren Hewett struck him as the pushy sort. Just the opposite in fact. Even back in high school, she had been so painfully shy that none of the guys paid her much attention. Travis thought he remembered hearing that she'd been traumatized by the death of her father and afterward devoted herself to her mother to the exclusion of developing a life of her own.

There was something rather touching in the way she had so self-consciously accepted that silly bouquet earlier that challenged his sense of chivalry. Even the hardest-hearted rogue would be moved to save a damsel in distress from Marsh's boat-size two left feet and endless self-aggrandizing. Dancing with Henry's new stepdaughter was the least Travis could do in the way of helping her feel more at ease on what he assumed had to be a difficult day for her.

"I'd be delighted," he lied.

He prayed that the band would strike up a lively

number. The way his luck was running, he figured that the two of them, covered in sticky punch, would dry together like glue during an agonizingly long waltz. Whatever the band played, he hoped Lauren didn't expect him to make polite small talk. A man far more comfortable in the solitude of the open range than in formal affairs requiring a suit and tie, Travis found an old worn pair of jeans and work boots suited him better. Had he not so much genuine respect for his father's old business partner and longtime friend Henry Aberdeen, he would have done his usual routine with the wedding invitation he'd received: tossed it in the trash and sent an expensive gift in lieu of attending.

His worst fears were realized when the band commenced to play a good old-fashioned, belt-buckle-polishing slow dance. A minute later Travis discovered that his partner actually had a lovely figure beneath all those filmy layers of fabric. Despite the fact that Lauren went out of her way to hide that from the rest of the world, he couldn't help but notice when his body reacted of its own volition to the soft, womanly curves pressed against him. Her body fit his so perfectly that it didn't take any stretch of the imagination to envision dancing horizontally with her.

It was a nice change to dance with someone who didn't feel like a stick in his arms. He'd never had any luck trying to convince Jaclyn—or any other woman for that matter—that most men really didn't buy into that dying heroin addict look that graced so many magazines. Full-figured women were never out of fashion in his book. Mentally clothing Lauren in the same white dress that Marilynn Monroe immortalized while standing over a city vent left him feeling suddenly more aroused than he'd like anyone to notice.

Rather than putting a respectable distance between them on the dance floor, Travis was drawn even closer by the scent of her perfume. In a room filled with an overwhelming assortment of fragrances ranging from cloying to girlish, Lauren smelled so good that it was all he could do to keep from burying his nose in the nape of her neck and indulging himself like a bee sampling the choicest flower.

Studying her up close, Travis discovered she had very nice features: wide-set eyes the color of emeralds, good cheekbones, silky dark hair pulled a little too severely away from a heart-shaped face and a generous mouth that curved up appealingly when she smiled. She just didn't accentuate those features the way other women—like his ex-wife Jaclyn—did spending hours making themselves presentable to the world. The fact that Lauren didn't appear to be that kind of high-maintenance woman was admirable in its own way.

Then again, Travis was paying Jaclyn an obscene amount of alimony each month and he had never given Lauren Hewett a second glance before today.

"I feel awful about ruining your shirt. You have to allow me to pay for your dry cleaning bill," she offered.

Travis protested that the offer was unnecessary, but she refused to accept no for an answer.

"Really, I insist. There's only one problem...."

Travis found the way she worried her lower lip between her teeth oddly mesmerizing. And unbelievably sexy. Feeling a stab of awareness in his belly, he stared at her hard as she continued in a halting voice.

"I'd tell you to mail me the bill, but I don't know where I'm going to be. All I know is that I won't be here much longer…."

Travis noticed Fenton out of the corner of his eye. He was waiting his turn at the edge of the dance floor, eager to take up where he'd left off before hurling his dance partner into another man's arms. Strangely enough, Travis wasn't nearly as ready to give up Lauren as he thought he would be at the beginning of the song. He steered her in the opposite direction.

"I've got to get out of here," she blurted out, looking almost claustrophobic.

Travis wondered how much champagne Lauren had consumed over the course of the afternoon.

"Are you sick?" he asked.

"And tired," she admitted, "of my life in general."

Once again Travis found himself staring into a pair of wide, hypnotic eyes and asking almost against his own free will, "I don't suppose there's anything I could do to help?"

Lauren hiccupped daintily.

"You could always marry me and put an end to this misery."

Travis stumbled. All of a sudden he understood exactly why poor old Marsh had fallen over his own feet and baptized Travis with punch. To date, it was the quickest proposal he'd ever received from a woman he barely knew.

His reaction caused Lauren to blush a furious shade of pink. Nervous laughter intended to underscore the fact that she had only been joking cracked beneath the strain of her explanation.

"Don't worry, I'm only teasing," she told him. "Short of committing to anything so drastic, you could always help me find a place to stay. Under the circumstances, I really don't want to stay in this house any longer, but the only rentals available in town look like they should be condemned."

Her eyes glistened with the hint of tears, chipping away at the wall Travis had worked so hard to erect around his heart. Feeling her tremble in his arms, he cursed his insensitivity. Clearly, Lauren wasn't nearly as accomplished at hiding her feelings as other women. She wore them right there on her puffy bridesmaid sleeves for everybody to see. He imagined that she was feeling particularly vulnerable today.

In fact, the last time Travis had seen such a defenseless creature, he'd been looking at it from behind the barrel of his Colt .45. And even though that pesky raccoon was destroying his mother's garden, he hadn't the heart to put it away. To add insult to injury, the darned thing was so happy to have continuing free reign of the backyard, it had practically adopted Travis as its master.

A warning signal exploded inside his head. Bells, lights and whistles all at the same time. Travis was a man who worked hard at keeping a wide emotional distance between himself and the opposite sex. Ever since his divorce, he tended to categorize the entire female gender as cold, calculating and manipulative. Somehow, it was hard to paint this plainspoken English teacher with the same broad strokes as the woman who had pulverized his pride and his wallet four and a half years ago.

Just because Lauren didn't strike him as either a gold digger or the kind of woman who would cheat on a man just for kicks, he hesitated to get involved with any woman who might easily mistake his kindness as something more. Especially someone who made him feel as though she intended to correct his grammar while attempting to waltz him down the aisle toward a waiting preacher.

Catching himself wondering how Lauren might look with her hair freed from that constraining bun, he fought the urge to undo the pins and run his fingers though her dark tresses. When she dropped her head against his shoulder and leaned against him for an instant, he was instantly transformed from a reluctant dance partner into her willing protector. Feeling the warmth of her breath against the crisp open collar of his shirt, he held her close as the final strains of the waltz faded away. When she looked up from the top of his shoes, he noticed that her eyelashes were suspiciously wet. Something hard inside his chest rolled over.

Setting aside his own paranoia for the moment, Travis did what any gentleman with a vacant mouse-infested cabin on his property would do. He rushed in for the rescue without thinking of the consequences of his actions.

"I actually might be able to temporarily solve your housing problem," he said, tipping her head up with the calloused pad of his thumb and falling once again into the verdant fields of those green eyes. "But I can assure you that I'm the last person in the world to help anybody find a husband."

Two

No one was more surprised when Lauren threw her arms around Travis's neck and kissed him in front of all the invited guests than apparently Lauren, herself.

Except maybe for Travis.

One minute he was doing his best to describe the modest little cabin next to his own house on the homestead that his grandfather staked out back when the government was eager to give away land to any hardy soul who could survive even one brutal Wyoming winter on it. And the next he was on the receiving end of a kiss that knocked him right out of his cowboy boots.

Had there been a single disinterested observer in the room, he or she might have dismissed the gesture as one of overwhelming gratitude mixed with too much champagne punch. In all actuality, Lauren did little more than press her mouth against Travis's for an instant before drawing away and turning an enchanting shade of pink.

Indeed, it was no open-mouth, long, drawn-out Hollywood kiss that left Travis wanting so much more. He never imagined that a brief sampling of those surprisingly sweet lips could destroy all his illusions about the prudish Ms. Hewett. She tasted of champagne and wild temptation. Behind that unadorned, bookish exterior lay a promise of passion. And the unexpected thought that she might be wearing something seductive under all that fabric was as intriguing to Travis as the kiss itself.

Dissatisfied with such a chaste peck, he was tempted to ravage her mouth with the kind of kiss that would let her know beyond all doubt that he was not a man to be toyed with. He wondered if the timid little mouse would run back to the safety of her hole. Or would such an inappropriate public display transform her into a virtual wild cat—and him into her eager prey?

Travis stood in the middle of the dance floor looking at Lauren as if he were seeing her for the very first time. It was his own startled reaction to her kiss, more than the act itself, that shook him to the very core of his being—a being who had obviously denied himself the pleasure of a woman's companionship for too long. Not that he could think of anyone else who had such a peculiar effect on him. All of a sudden Travis was feeling so hot that he wouldn't have been surprised if Fenton rushed over to put him out with another dousing of punch.

"When can I see it?"

For a moment Travis thought Lauren was actually making an indecent inquiry before realizing that she was just asking about the cabin that he said she could stay in until something better came along. A glance around the Victorian style living room of Barbara Aberdeen's house made him doubt whether the Spartan accommodations he had to offer would suit her sheltered daughter.

"Don't feel like you have to commit to anything until you've seen it," he warned her.

"All I ask is that it has indoor plumbing."

Lauren's hopeful smile reached a pair of eyes shining with excitement. Travis didn't want her laboring under any delusions.

"It was fitted with modern appliances a few years back, but I can't vouch for how clean it is. There's probably a layer of dust an inch thick coating everything."

"I'm no stranger to a mop and a dust rag," she assured him.

"The mice have set up housekeeping before you…."

Lauren didn't so much as flinch.

"I'll get a cat."

The least likely candidate in the entire world had just offered her an opportunity on a silver platter and she wasn't about to look that particular gift horse in the mouth. That she was mentally mixing her metaphors wasn't nearly as disturbing as the fact that her hormones were mucking up her common sense. She could only assume that Travis Banks was no more attracted to her than she herself was to Fenton Marsh.

Still, for a moment there, when she had so impetuously pressed her lips against his, she imagined feeling his heart leap against hers. With eyes half-closed she could almost hear the rhythm of his heart beating. The thought that she just might have shocked the local playboy put a silly grin on her face. Lauren had a mind to shock the entire community before she was done transforming herself from a caterpillar to a butterfly.

"When would you like me to pick you up so I can show you around the place?" Travis asked.

It pleased Lauren immensely that the young "lady" who had spoken so disparagingly about her earlier in the day happened to overhear that question. When Sylvia Porter's mouth flew open, Lauren was reminded of some luckless onlooker standing near enough to a slot machine that had just hit the jackpot to salivate over the money spilling onto the floor. She wondered if the silly goose would actually associate what sounded like a request for a date to the fact that Lauren had caught the bouquet she had so badly coveted.

Lauren wasn't nearly so superstitious herself. But she was ready to make some major changes in her life that required a leap of faith.

"Whatever time works best for you. Since school let out for summer just last week, I can be ready any time," she told Travis, doing her best to sound breezy.

"I'll be out of town for the rest of the weekend, but I can pick you up here first thing Monday morning," he replied.

It was perfect. That would give Lauren enough time

to see the wedding couple off and catch her breath before starting to pack her own bags. Unless the cabin was an absolute hovel, she wanted to move in as soon as possible. The nicest wedding gift she could think of giving her mother was her privacy when she returned from her honeymoon cruise.

"It's a date," she said, just loud enough for Sylvia to overhear.

Though Lauren was exhausted after driving her mother and Henry to the airport then returning home to clean up after the gala reception, her brain was too busy making plans to let her fall asleep easily that night. Standing before her closet, she studied her wardrobe with a critical eye. It seemed everything she owned was a tasteful blend of blue, black or beige. As much as she loved and admired her mother, shopping with her over the years had clearly limited Lauren's sense of adventure. All too often, she came home from a sale dressed like a much older woman.

Deciding there was no time like summer to reinvent herself without the added worry of what her students and colleagues might think, Lauren began piling stacks of her most matronly items to give to Good Will. The first article to go was a perfectly serviceable, lace-around-the-high-collar nightgown that her aunt Hattie had given her for Christmas. She might not be ready for a pink feather boa just yet, but she secretly longed for a satin negligee and matching robe to replace her old flannel one. Someday. For now she'd settle for getting rid of the unimpressive outfits populating her life. Soon, the pile included sedate cardigans, demure blouses, conservative skirts and well-below-the-knee dresses. The purge left just a few basics hanging on her closet but she felt more liberated than ever before.

And liberation called for a celebration. Alone in the house for the first time since she could remember, Lauren staged her first conscious act of rebellion against her boring, staid life by sleeping in the nude.

When she awoke from fitful sleep the next morning, she blamed her state of undress for an erotic dream about a man with thick blond hair and smoky-gray eyes the color of fog lifting from the Tetons....

That those eyes were just as impassable in real life as those mighty mountain peaks made no difference to the wanton creature in her dreams who did a whole lot more than simply brush her lips against his.

Lauren was not the type to count on her dreams as being anything more than wishful thinking. Still, when she called her friend Suzanne a little while later and confided that she was ready for a makeover, it was Travis she thought about making herself over for.

"It's about time!" Suzanne exclaimed. "Dust off your credit card, and I'll be right over."

The last of her girlfriends to get married, Suzanne Venice was not one to make light of Lauren's desire to make a new start for herself. A freethinker and true veteran of the working population, she was of the belief that a woman couldn't know what she really wanted in life until she reached thirty. Eager and ready to help, she arrived on Lauren's doorstep less than an hour later with a stack of fashion magazines. A young woman wearing a leather halter top and a denim miniskirt accompanied her.

Suzanne made the appropriate introductions.

"This is my niece Claire who's visiting for a few days. She just finished cosmetology school. I told her you were ready for something new and different."

Such a proclamation would have left a weaker woman trembling. Lauren's experience with beauticians was limited to Mrs. Castone who had been cutting her hair since she was in high school—as well as just about every blue-haired woman's in town. This left a goodly population of females in Pinedale looking much too much alike and sending the trendier among them elsewhere for a more modern do.

Claire's look was definitely modern. Spiked out in all directions, her blond hair reminded Lauren of a porcupine. That it actually looked becoming on the neophyte hairdresser was of some comfort. While Suzanne flipped through a stack of fashion magazines, Claire studied Lauren's face and hair with the intensity of a doctor performing her first surgery.

"Do ya trust me?" she asked, popping a wad of gum.

Lauren nodded dumbly and crossed her fingers behind her back as Claire positioned her in a chair in the middle of the kitchen and took a pair of scissors in hand.

"Not too short please," she implored, squeezing her eyes shut.

Her hair might not be the height of fashion, but Lauren was just a smidgeon vain about her thick tresses. A half an hour later, she opened her eyes to see the floor covered with piles of glossy dark locks. She almost screamed when she ran a hand along the back of her naked neck.

"It's fabulous!" Suzanne assured her.

Lauren felt her throat close around a knot of regret. She knew her friend would be equally complimentary if her niece had given her a GI buzz. Claire held a mirror up to her face.

"Well, what d'ya think?"

Lauren wasn't quite sure what to think. It was much shorter than she really wanted. Layered in the back for lift and tapered in the front to frame her heart-shaped face, the style did bring out the russet highlights of her hair. Longish bangs added femininity to a cut that few women could carry off without seeming somewhat mannish. It gave Lauren a pixie quality that made her look much younger and more stylish.

"I can show you how to spike it like mine if you want," Claire told her.

Lauren swallowed hard at the thought. Until this very moment she hadn't realized how much she had actually been hiding behind her long hair and conservative clothing.

"I like it just the way it is," she announced, surprised to actually mean it.

Smiling broadly, Suzanne rubbed her hands together in glee. "Now to bring out those gorgeous eyes of yours."

She pulled a small paper sack from her voluminous handbag and spilled its contents on the kitchen table. An assortment of cosmetics tantalized the eye. Lauren found them utterly daunting. For fear of looking as clownish as some of the girls in her high school classes, she generally limited her makeup selections to a layer of pale pink lipstick and a touch of mascara in a demure shade of brown to the tips of her eyelashes.

Today she gave herself over to her friend, gladly accepting Suzanne's help. Lauren committed herself to taking good mental notes. Gray eyeliner, a tasteful combination of taupe and teal eye shadow and an application of darker mascara did indeed bring out Lauren's eyes as promised. A dusting of blush also brought out a set of high cheekbones and a shocking mauve emphasized the fullness of a pair of lips that broke into a hesitant smile when Lauren surveyed the total effect of her makeover. The pixie in her mirror suddenly looked very grown-up.

She scarcely recognized herself.

"Now it's time to go clothes shopping," Suzanne announced.

Although the look on her friend's face reminded Lauren too much of Dr. Frankenstein for her liking, she was nevertheless grateful for the offer. Claire refused to take a penny for the haircut, saying that she would appreciate a positive word-of-mouth recommendation.

"I'll let you buy me a beer before I leave town though," she added as an afterthought as she gathered up her belongings and headed back to her aunt's house.

"It's a deal," Lauren promised.

All gratitude aside, she wasn't too terribly disappointed to hear that Claire would be unable to accompany them on their shopping expedition. If what Claire was wearing at the moment was any indication, she probably did most of her shopping at a hip, urban outfitters. As cute as the butterfly on the younger woman's right shoulder might be, Lauren didn't much care for the idea of being dragged into a tattoo parlor, either.

Suzanne wouldn't hear of patronizing any of the local clothing shops and insisted they drive to the trendy tourist town of Jackson Hole where boutiques proudly displayed one-of-a-kind designs for a clientele of movie stars and local millionaires. When Lauren expressed her concern about the cost of such a venture, her friend promptly put things into perspective.

"Chic doesn't come cheap. Besides, you don't have to buy out any one store. Just a few dynamite outfits will be well worth the investment. Hopefully the next time we go shopping it'll be for a wedding dress."

That promise was enough to convince Lauren to go for it. Having saved most of her salary by living at home for so long, she felt entitled to a frivolous spending spree. A couple of hours later she placed a stack of purchases on the counter of a place aptly named Diva's Digs. Only the thought of building a new life with a man who loved and appreciated her kept Lauren from complaining when the salesclerk rang up her purchases: an outrageously expensive pair of designer jeans, a brown checked sundress that made her feel rather like a debutante, a variety of leek tops, some classic tapered pants, matching shoes. And one timeless little black dress.

By the time they rolled back into town well after dark, Lauren felt like a movie star herself—a rather nervous movie star wondering when her leading man was going to make an appearance in her latest script....

As promised, Travis arrived bright and early Monday morning to take Lauren to his grandfather's old cabin to see if she was even slightly interested in renting it. Claiming that she would be doing him a favor by simply keeping the mice at bay, he had already offered it to her for free, but she wouldn't so much as think of staying there without paying something. Travis supposed she didn't want anyonΔe thinking that she was a "kept" woman or something equally archaic.

The thought brought a smile to his lips as he sauntered up the well-tended walk to Lauren's front door. He couldn't imagine anyone believing the conservative Ms. Hewett capable of such debauchery. After the wedding reception last Thursday, Travis had spent a little time thinking about that spontaneous kiss Lauren had given him. He'd finally come to the conclusion that he had greatly overestimated its impact. It was easy enough to blame his reaction on the fact that he had deprived himself of female company for too long. Having been taken by surprise, his testosterone had simply kicked into overdrive. He wouldn't let himself be so easily ambushed today.

When Lauren met him at the door, he couldn't have

been more startled than had she greeted him wearing absolutely nothing at all. Mouth open, he stared at her in confusion.

"What did you do different?" he blurted out with uncharacteristic lack of tact.

He wondered if she'd booked an appointment on one of those extreme makeover television shows. Surely a pair of pants couldn't make such an amazing change. The smile she gave him was nothing short of dazzling and made him feel somehow taller simply for having shown up on her doorstep.

"I cut my hair," she said simply enough. "Do you like it?"

"As a rule, I don't like short hair on women," he admitted honestly enough.

Nevertheless, Travis certainly found hers a tremendous improvement. He was struck by an urge to run his fingers though it and see if it really was as soft and shiny as it looked. Watching the corners of her lips turn from a smile to a frown, he realized too late that he had hurt her feelings. He hadn't meant to. His mother had raised him better than to insult a lady, and he hastened to remedy his blunder.

"It looks nice on you, though. In fact you look great."

Glad he didn't have to lie, he wondered if a haircut and new clothes could really transform this shy wallflower into a blossoming Cinderella. Finding no fairy godmother hovering in the near vicinity, Travis reminded himself that he was the last person in the world to question what a woman did to herself. His ex-wife had made it clear that any decision involving her own body was entirely the woman's prerogative.

Including whether or not she wanted to carry his baby....

Jaclyn wasn't one to strap herself to an endless pile of dirty diapers, or run after some ungrateful "rug rat." Never mind the fact that she'd claimed to be on birth control when she wasn't. Or that she'd used her pregnancy to force a proposal out of him in the first place. Or that she'd ultimately terminated it without his consent.

Travis had never felt so helpless in his whole life. Nor so angry.

Or hurt.

The memory of that tragic day swamped him. To this day, he had to turn away whenever he saw a father and son playing catch in the park. Or a dad teaching his "little princess" how to ride a bike. Or a happy young couple playing peek-a-boo with an infant. Sucked in by dark waters passing under the bridge of time, Travis tried to shake off his murky thoughts while waiting for Lauren to lock her front door behind her.

"Not many people around here bother with that," he observed.

"I know, but nowadays you have to be careful about who you trust."

Travis couldn't agree with her more. Reminding himself that sometimes monsters wore pretty, deceptive faces, he redoubled his efforts to give his heart the same consideration Lauren gave her mother's house. Such conscientiousness boded well for her reliability as a renter, but considering the isolation of his cabin, he assured her that such wariness would be completely unwarranted "out in the boonies."

A gentle breeze carried the delicate scent of her jasmine perfume as they walked to his pickup. Opening the passenger door of his one-ton dually for her, Travis realized it was a fragrance that could get under a man's skin. He hadn't been able to get it out of his mind since the reception, and right now it was making him itchy from the inside out.

Standing just under five foot five inches in her stocking feet, Lauren needed a stepladder to climb into the truck. Seeing as he didn't carry one around with him, Travis offered to help her up into the cab. He was glad she didn't object when he put his hands on either side of her waist and gave her a little boost. And relieved that she didn't slap him when they lingered there a moment longer than they should have.

Their gazes collided. Travis lost himself in a pair of eyes the color of aspen leaves at the first sign of spring. There was no softer color on the face of the earth. The air in his lungs got stuck there as he forgot to breathe.

Just the other day on the dance floor he'd had to fight his way through all those filmy layers of chiffon just to even find her waist. Today Lauren wasn't bothering to hide her mouthwatering physical attributes. A crop top the color of pale lemon meringue was tucked enticingly into a pair of slacks. There was nothing particularly sexy about the pants that Travis could see—other than the way they hugged her hips made him want to peel them off of her.

Whoa! This is no frivolous little swinger looking for a good time. This is a woman who's made no bones about the fact that she's looking to settle down. Hell, I'm not so sure she was joking earlier when she asked you to marry her. And you, cowboy, are about as eager to tie that knot again as somebody standing on the gallows....

With that solemn reproof in mind, Travis purposely worked at keeping the conversation light as they traveled the five miles out of town to the Half Moon Ranch. Nestled into the base of the mountains and dissected by a picturesque river, it had been in the Banks family for generations and meant everything to Travis. That land was as much a part of him as the marrow in his bones.

Against his lawyer's advice, Travis maintained that Jaclyn was welcome to anything she wanted in the divorce—except the ranch itself. A woman devoid of sentimentality or an appreciation of nature, Jaclyn had wanted to subdivide the property the instant she calculated its value by an investor's standard. She simply couldn't understand why anyone would endure the long hours and physical labor necessary to keep such a massive operation going when a killing could be made by selling it off. It hadn't taken her long to discover that the life of a rancher's wife was not the one of luxury that she'd expected. And to abandon it as quickly as she had her vows.

The scent of Lauren's perfume, with its own subtle, flirtatious voice, filled any lapses in the conversation and kept him from traveling too far down old roads. Lauren seemed so excited about the prospect of having her own place that she was oblivious to the effect she was having on him. Travis was glad he'd paid someone to come over on the weekend to straighten the place up. He didn't care whether Lauren actually rented it or not, but he didn't want her mocking that which held a special place in his heart. The times he had spent with his grandfather in that old cabin were among his best childhood memories.

He didn't need to worry. Lauren fell in love with it the moment she set eyes on it.

"It's perfect!" she exclaimed as if seeing the Taj Mahal instead of the humble little cabin that his ex-wife considered an eye sore.

Sentimental value, and a certain measure of spite, had kept Travis from complying with Jaclyn's repeated requests to tear it down. There was no denying that the place was a fixer-upper, but that only seemed to endear it to Lauren all the more. As she bubbled over with ideas on how to dress up the windows and what kind of furniture would be coziest in front of the rock fireplace, Travis couldn't help but grin at her enthusiasm.

She turned her back to gaze out the window at the Bridger Wilderness in a moment of reverie. The pristine peaks in the background had nothing on the silhouette with which she presented him. It was surprisingly hard to keep his arms from encircling her curvaceous figure and sharing the view with her.

"This window is the focal point of the living room,

don't you think? Would you mind if I pounded a few nails in the walls? If I promise to use only small ones?"

Travis knew how much it would have pleased Grandpa to see someone appreciate the place enough to pay it any kind of loving touch. Only a few hardy perennials that Grandma Banks had planted years ago still bloomed in a neglected window box. He wondered if Lauren would bother to pluck the weeds that were choking them out.

"Pound away," he said, fighting to keep his imagination from leading him to thoughts of undressing this woman right there on the old horsehair couch against the wall.

Lauren's eyes shone as she thanked him, promising to keep the integrity of the place intact when considering a decorating scheme.

Travis didn't think there was any way she could hurt the place. After all, those thick, old logs had weathered the years without giving up an ounce of character.

"You're welcome to keep any of the furniture here. If you're sure you want to move in, I'll haul anything you don't want to the dump. It's been so long since anyone lived here, I can't even guess what your electric bill will be. As little square footage as there is, it can't be much."

Not one to quibble over the price of answered prayers, Lauren brushed off his concerns with yet another blinding smile. The wink she gave him was so unexpectedly playful that it caught Travis off guard and left him wondering if he hadn't, in fact, imagined it.

"Don't worry about that. Hopefully, I'll be out of here by the time winter rolls around since I only plan on being here until I'm married."

Three

As odd a look as Travis gave her, Lauren might as well have told him that she was catching a ride on the next spaceship to Mars. That he was so taken aback by her announcement was insulting. For the first time all day, she stiffened in his presence. She may not measure up to the supermodel types with whom he was rumored to cavort, but over the past few days she had come to the conclusion that a man could do worse than be seen around town with her.

"I didn't even know you were engaged," Travis stammered.

Lauren waved her hand as if dismissing something inconsequential.

"I'm not. Yet."

A firm believer in the force of language, she subscribed to the concept that a person's words shaped her future. That is, if she were to ask God for help and accepted what came about as a natural consequence of that prayer, Lauren liked to think that everything she needed would come to her at the perfect time. With her mother firmly entrenched in a new life, Lauren was ready to ask a generous universe to bestow upon her the man of her dreams. Whoever was sent to her didn't have to be particularly good-looking or have lots of money. She just wanted to finish out the rest of her days with a gentle and kind man who loved children and appreciated a good woman. Too bad if Travis Banks was above such humble dreams.

"Don't worry," she said dryly, hoping to wipe the stricken look from his face with the same flirtatious sense of humor that had seemed to work earlier. "I can't say that I've met the lucky man yet. But I believe the secret of success is a good set of plans."

Looking relieved to hear that he wasn't presently in the crosshairs of her sights, he assumed the air of an amused Southerner as he drawled, "Why, Ms. Hewett, are you telling me that you are planning to entertain gentlemen callers on the property?"

Without missing a beat, Lauren batted her eyelashes at him in gross exaggeration. But the tone she employed was thoroughly modern. "That is exactly what I'm telling you. Do you have a problem with that?"

Her directness was disconcerting. Travis was surprised to feel a slight sense of relief to hear that she wasn't engaged yet. Since he seriously doubted that a woman of Lauren's sterling reputation was going to be throwing wild parties any time soon, he had no qualms about handing the key over to her—other than the fact that he hadn't been able to get her out of his mind ever since she'd laid that harmless little kiss on him a couple of days ago.

"Of course not," he assured her with a wink of his own. "You can turn the place into a playgirl mansion for all I care."

Ignoring the blunt edge of his verbal irony, Lauren held out her hand to accept the key he offered. Freedom glinted off its brassy surface. Five miles out of town may not be enough to keep the local gossipmongers quiet, but it should be far enough away to give her a sense of privacy and autonomy.

Her own place! What a sweet refrain those words were to a woman striking out on her own for the very first time. A world that only a few short days ago seemed parochial and plodding in its predictability suddenly sparkled with endless possibilities like so many diamonds glittering against a jeweler's black velvet display cloth.

Lauren was quiet on the ride back to town, her mind too preoccupied with decorating plans to notice the way Travis kept casting surreptitious glances her way. He had certainly made himself clear enough on the matter of his precious bachelor status for her to disregard him as a potential suitor. Aside from the fact that he reacted the way a skittish colt did around a man with a heavy saddle whenever the subject of marriage came up, Travis Banks wasn't exactly what Lauren would consider good husband material.

Just because he'd always had the power to turn her insides to mush whenever she looked at him didn't mean she couldn't separate rational thought from foolish fantasy. For one thing, he carried too much baggage from an apparently painful past relationship. For another, he was too handsome and sure of himself for his own good. Still insecure about her own appearance, Lauren didn't like the thought of having to compete with the rest of womankind for a man's attention. She liked even less the possibility of marrying someone who might very well cheat on her the minute someone prettier threw herself in his way. Lastly, a real cowboy like Travis would probably care more for his livestock than he did for any woman.

That settled in her mind, she turned to him as a confidant.

"Would you mind telling me where the best place in town is to pick up single men?"

Travis swerved to miss a jackrabbit.

"You mean other than church or the local Laundromat?" he asked.

Lauren rolled her eyes.

"I mean like a bar."

From his reaction, one would think she was inquiring about a male escort service. Lauren refused to look away. If anyone would know the answer to that question surely it was the most eligible single man in these parts. After that jab about turning his grandpa's cabin into the playgirl mansion, she saw no reason why he shouldn't be completely forthright with her.

"The Alibi," he said grudgingly. "If all you're looking for is a one-night stand, that is."

She wasn't, but since Lauren was long past the age of having a coming out party, she could think of no better way to announce her intentions to the world than circulating in the most happening spots. In a small community, when one got stereotyped as a stick in the mud as far back as high school, drastic measures were required. And just because she might let a friendly guy buy her a drink certainly didn't mean she had to go to bed with him. Marriage, not gratuitous sex, was her ultimate goal—although she sincerely hoped a good deal of the latter was thrown in with the former.

"There's a church social scheduled for this weekend if you're interested," Travis suggested.

Lauren's pulse leaped at the thought that he might actually be asking her to accompany him, but his overly nonchalant tone convinced her that she was mistaken. An unexpected wave of disappointment washed over her. Having allowed him to step all over her pride since before he'd even known she existed, she vowed not to let it happen. Besides, she'd been to enough staid church socials to know that the only eligible men in attendance were either horny teenagers or widowers collecting Social Security. Determined to shed her heavy cloak of invisibility once and for all, she tipped her chin defiantly up.

"I'm really not."

A more experienced woman might have been better able to read the frustration in Travis's face. As it was, Lauren simply tuned him out by turning her head to stare out the window and proceeded to shade her eyes against a future so bright it threatened to burn her if she wasn't careful.

Travis was duly impressed with his tenant's industriousness. Lauren took him up on his offer to take a load of old furniture that she didn't want to the dump. By the time he returned she was in the process of polishing the old hardwood floors until they gleamed. With a gingham kerchief holding her hair away from her face, she looked the picture of domestic industry. On her hands and knees, she presented an enticing view that put the most indecent thoughts into his head. He struggled to find his voice.

When he cleared his throat to announce himself, Lauren's hand flew to her hair as though in embarrassment at being found in such a disheveled state. Travis hoped she thought that was the reason why he turned down her offer of a homemade lunch rather than discover the real reason he was in such a hurry to flee. Lacing his hands nonchalantly over the bulge in his jeans, he backed out the front door with all the grace of a teenage boy ill at ease with his sexuality.

The following day, he watched from the safety of his own front porch as she replaced all the old, faded curtains with a feminine, although not overly fussy, print.

When the furniture store dropped off a new couch and bed, Travis couldn't help but notice how long the deliverymen lingered on the porch sipping the fresh squeezed lemonade Lauren offered them. For some perverse reason, Travis took pleasure in the fact that one man's hair was thinning and he sported a paunch. However, he found himself scowling when he caught the younger of the two rolling up the sleeves of his shirt to reveal an impressive set of biceps as he helped her open a window that was stuck—a simple task that Travis himself would have been more than happy to have done for her if she had only thought to ask him.

From the relatively short distance separating their places, he could see the warmth of Lauren's smile as she refilled the guy's glass not once, but twice. Travis couldn't get over how different she was looking these days. It wasn't just her new haircut and an artful application of makeup that made a man take notice, either. There was a new bounce in her step, a waggle in her wiggle that Travis hadn't remembered seeing before.

Watching her stretch those long legs of hers out to their full length in a pair of shorts as she attempted to hang a porch glider from the overhang the very next day didn't do anything to make him feel any less a voyeur. If Lauren Hewett ever discovered the effect her body could have on a man, she just might be dangerous. For the life of him, Travis didn't know why he'd even mentioned such an infamous spot as the Alibi to her earlier. Ever since bringing it up, he'd been praying she would just forget it and opt for the church social instead. He hoped Lauren was too caught up in the process of red-ecorating that old cabin to have enough energy left over to get herself into too much trouble.

He figured wrong.

Lauren checked her reflection in the mirror one last time before dabbing perfume behind each earlobe and heading for town. She was so apprehensive about go-ing into a bar alone that she'd called on Suzanne for moral support. Unfortunately, her makeover buddy had been forced to decline due to a previous engagement, but she most graciously offered to send her niece in her place. They met up in the parking lot outside the bar shortly after nine o'clock.

Wearing the exact same outfit she'd had on when she'd cut Lauren's hair, Claire was undaunted by the sight of the usual crew at The Alibi. In fact, she seemed inordi-nately pleased by the loud whistles and "yee-haws" that accompanied their arrival. That an equal number of mo-torcycles and pickups filled the lot was enough to put the local police force on alert. A patrol car parked out front did nothing to deter a multitude of lonely cowboys and oil field workers from crowding into the smoke-filled bar with loving on their minds and paychecks burning holes in their pockets.

A bouncer sporting a tattoo of a skull and crossbones across an arm as big as a cottonwood branch admitted Lauren and Claire with a smile that showed off his gold tooth. In her chic sundress, Lauren looked as out of place in the honky-tonk as he might at a high tea. Surveying her from head to toe in an overtly masculine gesture, he gave her a look as if to ask if she were lost.

"There's no cover charge," he said. "It's ladies' night tonight."

It was definitely a misnomer for the clientele that frequented The Alibi. Men outnumbered the women by a goodly five-to-one margin.

"I like the odds," Claire said, putting a hand to the middle of Lauren's back and pushing her inside.

Once they were in the bar, Claire grabbed the closest chair and lit up a cigarette.

As tempted as Lauren was to ask her to extinguish it, she didn't want to insult her companion. The bar was so smoky that such a request would be like trying to keep the chlorine in one half of a swimming pool with a fishing net. Blinking, she gave her eyes time to adjust to the dimness of the room and strained to hear Claire over the deafening roar of a band that was clearly more into volume than producing a quality sound.

"Tequila!" the crowd shouted along with the refrain of the song that the band was in the midst of playing.

Lauren began tapping her foot in time with the music. The place was packed. Unable to catch the barmaid's attention on her own, she was surprised when a young lady wearing an apron longer than her skirt sauntered over to their table with two tall drinks.

"From a couple of admirers," she said, setting them down.

The drinks were so strong that Lauren thought the bartender must have forgotten to put any soda in hers.

Accustomed as she was to being invisible, she didn't quite know how to react to all the attention suddenly being directed her way. Men were straining their necks to get a better look.

Claire was more than willing to help her enjoy the moment.

"Drink up," she said, clinking their glasses together and giving the eye to a couple of good-looking hustlers chalking up their cue sticks at a nearby pool table. "Tequila!"

"The woman has the common sense of a goose," Travis muttered under his breath. Perched on a bar stool, he had a slightly elevated view of all the comings and goings in the shabby bar. He reminded himself that he'd stopped by just for a quick drink, not to check up on his renter's whereabouts. Definitely not. It wasn't exactly like he'd followed her to The Alibi shortly after watching her leave from his living room window. He'd simply had a hankering to go to town right about that same time.

Damn, but Lauren looked sexy in that soft, flared dress with the ridiculously wide belt that emphasized her trim waist. Matching shoes and handbag were wasted upon the other men leering at her from surrounding tables. A smart guy would simply leave her to her own matchmaking devises, however poorly thought out they were.

Despite a word of warning to himself that he wasn't anyone's keeper, his adrenaline kicked in along with his protective instincts as he overheard a suggestive remark about his naive tenant from someone walking past. Reminding himself that it hadn't been intended for him to hear, he unclenched his fist and took a sip of beer. The sooner he got her out of here the better. If Lauren wasn't of a mind to leave just yet, he'd just park himself at her table and scare off the more menacing sorts until she was ready to go.

He was in the process of unhitching his boots from his stool when a big cowboy tipped his hat in Lauren's direction and made his move to cash in on the drinks he'd bought the two women earlier. Travis shouldn't have been so surprised to see that Lauren could hold her own on the dance floor. Anyone who could survive a two-step with Fenton Marsh should manage well enough with the kind of men who frequented The Alibi. Such hard-drinking skirt chasers were often deceptively light on their feet.

Travis watched closely to make sure no one slipped anything into her drink. Unfortunately, date rape drugs were no longer confined to big cities.

He saw her laugh as her partner spun her around, caught her in the crook his arm and dipped her precariously close to the floor. As the final strains of the song died away, Travis could hear her deep-throated laugh and watched in disgust as men lined up like dominoes for an opportunity to gain her affection. Had Lauren known the score, it might have been amusing to watch, but he doubted she could figure that particular number with a preprogrammed calculator. She didn't have the chance to make it back to her table before another guy tapped her on the shoulder and asked her for the next dance.

"The lady's with me," the big cowboy grumbled threateningly.

Because Lauren was after maximum exposure tonight, hoping to get her name circulating among the single men in the community, she wasn't about to limit herself to just one suitor so early in the evening. She smiled sweetly at the cowboy who'd bought both Claire and her yet another round of drinks so that it would be hard for him to think he'd wasted his money.

"I'll save the next dance for you," she promised.

While Lauren had been dancing, Claire had connected with one of the pool players who'd caught her eye and now was leaving with him. Lauren waved goodbye as she made her way back to a table now loaded down with a wide assortment of drinks. She was startled to see Travis sitting there frowning at her.

"Grab your coat," he growled, scooting his chair right up next to hers so he didn't have to scream to make himself heard. "I'm taking you home."

Thinking he was worried that her friend had left her stranded, she hastened to assure him. "I have my own vehicle."

She enunciated each word carefully so he wouldn't suspect that she'd had a teensy bit too much to drink already. The best cure for that, she was sure, was to burn off any excess alcohol on the dance floor.

"You can leave your car here overnight."

Wondering why her powers of invisibility were suddenly failing to protect her from someone who'd never hesitated to look through her before, Lauren shook her head to the contrary. Not wanting to appear ungrateful for all the money that had been spent on her over the course of an hour, she took a sip from every drink lined up in front of her. The variety of alcohol was working its way though a body unused to more than an occasional glass of sherry during the holidays.

Travis was feeling the heat of at least half a dozen other men glaring at him. He fixed a deceptively neutral smile on his face. He'd timed his request for Lauren to get out of Dodge to coincide with Ox's trip to the bathroom, and her stubborn refusal to leave while she was having so much fun was jeopardizing his careful planning.

"Stick around, doll," interjected a swarthy guy from the next table. "I'll take you home whenever you want."

Barely an inch separated the man's head from his shoulders.

Travis's muscles tensed. Whether Lauren knew it or not, she was in way over her head. If his own sister Callie ever found herself in such a predicament, he hoped to hell someone would step in and save her from herself. Of course with spitfire Callie the likelihood was that somebody just might need to save the stranger *from* her.

Still, Travis would never forgive himself if a woman came to harm and he'd stood by and done nothing to prevent it. His mother had drummed it into his head that it was a man's obligation to protect a lady. No matter how crazy that lady might be acting....

A meaty hand came down on Lauren's shoulder.

"Forget it, buddy. She's going home with me," a hostile voice announced from behind Travis.

Apparently having finished up his business in the men's room, the cowboy was not at all happy with the prospect of being shot out of the saddle. Though not as stocky and compact in build as this one, the guy at the next table was by no means a weakling. When he stood up to kick his chair out of the way, Travis recognized him as Toss Weaver. He had come by his name in this very establishment—by tossing a competitor in a strong man competition across the ring. To this day the other man remained disabled.

Toss's favorite way of provoking a fight was to knock a Stetson off some drunk cowboy's head and stomp it into the ground. As a preventative measure, Lauren's suitor took off his hat and set it in the middle of the table.

"There's no reason to—" Lauren began to say.

"Shut up!" Toss said, not so much as glancing at her.

That was as far as Travis was willing to let things go. Dropping a hand beside his thigh, he grabbed the leg of Lauren's chair and, doing his best to avoid drawing attention to the act, dragged them both several feet back from the table. Having suffered more than his fair share of black eyes over the years in the name of chivalry, Travis wasn't particularly inclined to step between two giants who looked as though they belonged in a Grimm's fairy tale.

A second later, the cowboy lunged over the table. Beer flew everywhere. Taking hold of Lauren by the wrist, Travis pulled her out of her chair.

"What do you think you're doing?" she protested.

So much for the eternal gratitude of a damsel in dis-

tress, Travis thought as he hauled her out of harm's way, a direction that happened to take them toward the dance floor.

The sound of vile swearing, tables breaking and glass shattering immediately drew a crowd. Unfazed, the band played on, if anything more loudly than before. Tightening his grip, Travis swung his free arm around Lauren with the easy familiarity of a man claiming his woman. Then he unobtrusively proceeded to waltz her around the few remaining couples on the dance floor toward the back door. A siren wailed out front.

"But shouldn't we—"

Travis cut the question off by gently pressing her head against the hollow of his shoulder. He rested his cheek against her hair and inhaled the scent that had haunted him since the last time she'd worn it for his benefit. It was far more intoxicating than anything he'd had to drink.

Lauren snuggled up against him and followed his lead. Considering her alcohol consumption for the evening, she moved well to the beat of the music. That she felt even better than she smelled said a lot for his restraint at the moment.

"This is nice," she murmured.

Goose bumps rose along Travis's neck. A dimly lit exit sign glowed through the haze of cigarette smoke less than a dozen steps away. He barely had time to react to the surge of tenderness that welled up in his heart and sent an unmistakable tingling sensation to a part of his body even less inclined to follow the rules of logic.

Cool air hit them both in a refreshing blast as Travis maneuvered his way out of the hot bar and into the night. Cat eyes that seemed more magical every time he looked into them widened in surprise as Lauren realized with a start that she was no longer inside. It was hard to think that just a couple of days ago Travis had considered this woman plain. Then again, a couple of days ago he'd also acted out of a sense of almost brotherly concern when he'd offered to rent Lauren a place for next to nothing.

Studying her flushed face in the glow of the moon and the reflection of flashing police car lights arriving on the scene, Travis realized with a start that he was no longer feeling the least bit fraternal toward this woman. And that was far more intimidating to him than any Neanderthal who might be waiting for him inside the bar.

Four

Not quite sure what to make of the feelings she stirred in him, Travis grumbled, "Lady, why is it I always end up with drinks spilled all over me whenever you're even close to a dance floor?"

Lauren leveled a scowl at him. "Maybe because you keep getting in my way."

Travis took a step back. After risking life and limb for her, he couldn't believe Lauren actually had the audacity to be angry *with him*. Thinking he could coax an apology out of her, he tried making his point with sarcasm.

"Given the way you're feeling, I take it that a thank-you is out of the question then?" he asked.

Lauren's eyes glittered. "For what? Cutting my evening short?"

Too much of a gentleman to simply walk away and leave her to catch a ride home in the back of a cop car, Travis was nonetheless tempted to let Pinedale's finest see if they could talk any sense into this confounding woman. One minute Ms. Lauren Hewett was as bland as vanilla pudding, the next so damned hot half the men in town were crawling and brawling all over her. And she was treating him as if he were some kind of wet blanket. It was too damned bad that Lauren didn't realize she should be grateful that he was around to keep a watchful eye out for her. That he cared enough to stick his neck out on her behalf. That he'd rushed to her rescue.

"For saving your virtue for starters," he ventured to explain.

Given his usual nonjudgmental attitude toward sex, those words sounded stilted even to his own ears. He knew what century this was. Maybe he thought such old-fashioned values would appeal to the type of woman he'd always assumed Lauren was. Maybe he just needed to believe that there was at least one single woman left on the planet worthy of being placed on a pedestal.

But Lauren didn't think twice about jumping off that shining platform and hitting him full in the face with her own version of reality.

"It isn't my virtue that's in jeopardy, you fool! It's my future."

Travis shook his head at the benign insult she hurled at him. She looked mad enough to march straight back into that full-blown barroom fray just to prove her point. He had to fight back a grin at the thought of her taking on Toss Weaver single-handedly—and winning. When Travis put a restraining hand on her elbow, she threatened him with the kind of seething look that had the power to quiet an entire room of rowdy students.

"Listen," she explained in a rush of exasperation that actually ruffled her bangs. "I suppose you think I should feel indebted to you for 'saving' me in there. But the truth of the matter is I had more fun tonight than I can remember having in a long, long time. Maybe it's wrong of me to feel a tiny thrill that a couple of brawny guys actually got into a fight over me, but I can guarantee you it was a whole lot more exciting than anything that was going to happen at the church social tonight."

Captivated by the sparkle in those green eyes, Travis nonetheless felt obliged to point out the most obvious flaw in her logic.

"Your plan to march one of those drunken cavemen to the altar would work better in Vegas," he snapped. "Here, it'll just lead to a cheap hotel room or the back seat of a car parked far enough out of town so that nobody can hear your screams."

Shaken by the warning and hurt by Travis's assumption that she was desperate enough to marry just *anybody,* Lauren fumbled for the keys in her purse.

"Why don't you just let go of my arm and any preconceived notions about my virtue before you tuck yourself in for the night?" she snapped.

Her words were slightly slurred, and Travis questioned her articulation of the word "tuck." Whatever insults she hurled at him didn't warrant letting her behind the wheel of a car in her condition.

"Friends don't let their renters drive drunk," he mumbled to himself.

Lauren jerked her arm out of his grasp.

"Let go of me!"

The confrontational act drew a nearby policeman's attention. The next thing Travis knew the officer was heading in their direction, presumably to check out the typical domestic disputes that occur outside of bars late at night. Keeping a cool head about him, Travis did what he had to do to quell any suspicions that Lauren needed to be saved *from* him.

He kissed her.

An act intended only to shut her up blossomed into something far less practical as Lauren proceeded to dissolve in his arms. Travis had been preoccupied with kissing her again ever since she'd shocked him with that sweet little peck at the wedding reception. Seizing the opportunity to simultaneously satisfy his curiosity and allay the officer's concern, he cradled the back of her head in one hand, covered her mouth with his own and effectively stifled any protest she might have been about to make.

She tasted even sweeter than he remembered. But behind that sweetness burned a red-hot appetite. Far away from the constraints of proper society, Lauren yielded to his demands without a fight. The teacher proved an apt pupil, letting out a tiny gasp of surprise when Travis's tongue parted her lips and exacted a full response from her. As her gasp quickly turned to a satisfied moan, a stab of desire pierced his groin.

The kiss was purely sexual, wet and full of reckless desire. And it happened so fast that Lauren simply responded.

With every ounce of her being.

Melting against him, she inadvertently forced him to pull her so snugly against the length of his body that there was no doubt left just what power she exercised over him. Mating her tongue against his, she stoked the fire that threatened to destroy all rational thought and made it impossible for him to turn back. Travis tightened his grip around her waist at the thought of some bully from the bar taking advantage of her. A surge of possessiveness engulfed him as he proceeded to devour her.

It wasn't the night air alone putting goose bumps on Lauren's bare arms. Nor the alcohol making the ground move beneath her feet. She had dreamed of this moment since she was a dewy-eyed freshman in high school. But none of her adolescent fantasies measured up to the reality of kissing Travis Banks. Achingly, painfully wonderful, his kisses defied description.

Lauren didn't notice the streetlamp dimming in seeming deference to the electricity arcing between them. Nor did she pay any attention to the fact that her expensive little purse slipped from her grasp and found a home at her feet. She was too preoccupied with the way Travis's big, masculine hands were so thoroughly exploring her curves and turning her bones to liquid.

How his tongue explored the inner texture and curve of her lips. How hers slid in and out of his mouth, sharing the taste of fine whiskey and making her feel light-headed and giddy.

Pressed against the hard plane of his chest, her breasts tingled, and her nipples hardened into tight buds. Blood pounded in her ears, and a demanding primal sensation tugged at the muscles of her belly. Her knees turned to jelly. She tried steadying herself by wrapping her arms around Travis's chest but discovered that she could not lace her fingers together to span its impressive width. Raising her arms to let them rest on his broad shoulders, she feathered fingers through hair as silky as his kisses. By the time he had his fill of her, Lauren felt perfectly ravaged.

Perfectly.

When finally Travis pulled away, he took a deep breath before resting his chin on the top of her head. A purr of pleasure rumbled against Lauren's throat as she braced her hands against his chest. Heat radiated from beneath a shirt damp with sweat, and she felt the play of muscles under her fingers before finally letting her arms fall to her sides.

Travis waved at the policeman who had been stopped in his tracks by the amorous display. "Everything's under control over here, Officer."

Having felt his heart beating so wildly against her own, Lauren was not fooled by the remark. Travis was no more under control than she was. A bubble of feminine pride caught in her chest at the telltale bulge behind the button fly of his jeans.

By the time she retrieved her purse, their conscientious policeman had returned to his squad car and turned his attention to less lusty matters—like assisting an enraged Toss Weaver into the back seat of his free "tipsy taxi." The effects of too many sips from too many drinks combined with the lingering intoxication of Travis's kisses left Lauren ready to call it a night. It would be pointless to go back into the bar now thinking she could possibly find anyone who could kiss better than the man who still had his arms around her. Putting a hand to her head, she tried to steady the world swimming about her.

Suddenly meek she asked, "Are you sure you wouldn't mind taking me home?"

Travis stated the obvious with a relieved smile. "You're right on my way, darling."

He guided Lauren over to his pickup, opened the door for her, swept her off her feet and proceeded to set her into the front seat as easily as he might a rag doll. He then grabbed the seat belt and dragged it across the front of her body to buckle her in. His touch burned through her clothes. Completely innocuous in nature, the act of his forearm brushing against the swell of her breast felt so very intimate that it sucked the breath right out of Lauren's lungs. She attempted to resuscitate herself while Travis walked around the vehicle and settled himself behind the wheel.

Despite the cool night temperature and the fact that the heater was shut off, the air in the vehicle was warm, charged by some unknown completely unpredictable force.

"Do you mind if I turn on the radio?" he asked.

"By all means."

Travis might need the noise to keep him from falling asleep, but Lauren had never felt more alive and awake in her life. She was too pumped up by the events of the evening to so much as close her eyes.

Sexual tension crackled like the static accompanying the country song playing on the radio. She studied the masculine hands draped over the steering wheel. Hands that propelled a football so powerfully down a field all those many years ago were scarred by hard physical labor. Everyone knew Travis to be a wealthy man. Lauren always thought of him as a gentleman rancher who parceled out the most demanding jobs to his hired hands. Scrutinizing those hands that she had once fantasized all over her body made Lauren realize that she had grossly oversimplified his life since she knew him in high school.

Resting her head against the leather seat back, she ventured where angels dared to tread.

"Do you mind telling me exactly what happened between Jaclyn and you? Everyone thought the two of you were the perfect couple."

Jaclyn had been model-thin and gorgeous. Polished and sophisticated. Lauren couldn't imagine a scenario in which two such beautiful people faced any problem so insurmountable that it ended in divorce. The silence that followed her question was long but not particularly sharp.

"I guess we just wanted different things," Travis finally answered under cover of darkness. "Different lives."

Though his words were spoken softly, they failed to hide the bitterness he felt over his failed marriage. He surprised himself by continuing.

"In the end, we couldn't seem to agree about anything."

"Like what?"

Travis sighed.

"Like whether children are a blessing or a curse. Whether Wyoming is heaven or hell on earth. Whether or not she could make me jealous. Whether marriage is a true partnership or a license to change one another. And whether any amount of money could ever settle our differences."

"I guess that's what they call irreconcilable differences," Lauren said in a small voice. It hurt her to hear the angst and self-recrimination in his voice, and she wished there was something she could say to lessen his pain. She wondered which of them had been opposed to having children.

"That's what the divorce papers said, and I'd just as soon leave it at that as pick away at the scars looking for blame."

Though Travis had barely scratched the surface of his complicated relationship, Lauren recognized his anguish in the way he gripped the steering wheel so tightly that it made his knuckles turn white by the dim glow of the dashboard lights. Impressed that he hadn't used the opportunity to vilify his ex-wife like so many divorced men who enjoy wallowing in that game, she was moved to reach across the seat and pat Travis's leg reassuringly. The harmless gesture sent a frisson of electricity through her entire body, reminding her that the man she used to dream of was no figment of her imagination but truly made of flesh and blood.

Just like her.

Travis took a hand from the steering wheel to cover the one resting on his thigh.

"Darlin', do you have any idea what you're doing to me?"

Torn from a throat raw from secondhand cigarette smoke, the question held a tacit threat.

And an unspoken promise…

For the second time that evening he addressed her by the endearment. Both times it reduced her to a puddle of goo. Supposing that he flung that word carelessly at many women, Lauren reminded herself for the hundredth time that this outspoken bachelor wasn't the settling down kind of man that she was looking for. Just because her long-ago crush called her "darling" didn't mean she should go throwing away a well laid out plan for her future on a night of cheap thrills.

Except that Travis didn't make her feel cheap. He made her feel like a precious object worthy of being protected at all costs. That he had rushed in to rescue her from a couple of liquored-up strongmen, albeit unnecessarily, indicated he wasn't trying to take advantage of her.

Since she refused to respond to the question he'd posed to her, Travis answered it himself by dragging her hand up his thigh and guiding it to the juncture between his legs. Lauren struggled for composure when he covered the swollen bulge there with her hand.

"Just in case you don't know, here's all the proof you need."

As tempted as Lauren was to pull her hand away, she was equally tempted to leave it right where it was and see how long it would take to force him to either pull over or wreck. Torn between wanting to discard the good-girl image that had long held her hostage and her desire for a committed relationship with a loving man, she didn't know what to do. Never in her wildest dreams had she imagined herself fondling Travis Banks as he drove her home—a mere stone's throw away from his sprawling ranch house. Leaving her hand right where he had put it, Lauren moved closer and decided to satisfy her curiosity once and for all.

Women could downplay size all they wanted, but Lauren grew positively wet at the thought of having something so big and hard inside her. Lordy, it was a wonder he didn't pop the rivets off those form-fitting jeans. That she could make such a man groan aloud was heady stuff.

Lauren hadn't returned home from college all those years ago a virgin, but her experience with men was limited, to say the least. And while she'd had a good time at the bar tonight, she hadn't wanted to so much as kiss any of the men with whom she'd danced. Certainly none made her want to rip off her clothes, discard her inhibitions and hop into bed with him.

Except for Travis.

The pickup swerved dangerously, and he yanked the steering wheel sharply to guide it back on the road. Headlights illuminated the open archway of the vast Half Moon Ranch. Frustration and relief laced his words as he announced in a tight voice, "We're home."

Could there be any sweeter words to a woman longing for a relationship with a good man? More than mere walls and flooring and a roof, *home* evoked images of a cozy fire in the hearth, the smell of freshly baked bread, wild roses on the table, primitive artwork displayed on the refrigerator and the sound of children's laughter floating through an open door. Lauren wished there was some way to let Travis know she wanted so much more than the simple physical satisfaction that both their bodies were demanding.

"One can only hope," she whispered, never dreaming that he might actually hear, let alone respond to, her heart's desire.

Five

Travis accompanied Lauren to her front door in stunned silence. The heartfelt words she'd whispered left him feeling like scum for allowing his thoughts to turn down such a purely carnal road. All Lauren wanted was a home, a husband and children to call her own. She'd never made any bones about that.

And cad that he was, all Travis could think about was how just getting this woman in and out of his pickup was proving to be almost as erotic as those persistent fantasies about getting her into his bed. In her present condition, Lauren had practically poured herself into his arms when he opened the passenger door and offered to see her safely inside. The warmth of her lovely, limp body pressed against his was enough to make a strong man weak. In such a compromising position, Lauren would have to be completely passed out not to notice he was as hard as a rock. He hadn't wanted a woman this badly since he'd been a horny teenager with more imagination than experience beneath his belt.

The trouble with acting on that powerful tug of arousal was that Travis was nowhere near ready to make the kind of commitment Lauren wanted. The very honesty that compelled her to blurt out her intentions of finding a husband before the first snow of the season would send most self-respecting bachelors scurrying for cover. He was as committed to retaining his single status as Lauren was to terminating hers. Having previously been burned by the institution of marriage and one very selfish and manipulative woman in particular, Travis wasn't inclined to make the same mistake again. Not that he was ready to forswear the female species all together.

Just those with big green eyes who believed in fairy-tale endings complete with fancy wedding gowns.

Travis considered that all too symbolic white dress. The likelihood of a woman of Lauren's age being a virgin was highly improbable.

"Would you like to come in?" she asked.

More than I care to admit.

"I really shouldn't," he said. Inhaling the scent of her delicate perfume, Travis donned a casual manner. "But I wouldn't mind taking a look at what you've done with the place."

He stepped inside, and Lauren fumbled for the light switch. Travis couldn't believe his eyes as they adjusted to the sudden glow. The change was amazing. For a woman who didn't plan on sticking around long, Lauren certainly had put in a lot of work into fixing up the once spartan cabin.

Soft blue cushions on white wicker furniture invited him to sit down and put his feet up. Scattered on the gleaming hardwood floor were several handwoven rugs in a Native American design. Matching curtains fluttered against a window open to the night air, and a bouquet of sunflowers added a bright spot of color against aged log walls. An array of breakable knickknacks straight from a magazine personalized the space. A moveable island made of pine expanded the limited kitchen work area.

Beauty and efficiency lay in the loving details of her decorating touches.

"Grandpa would love this," Travis said.

Though his grandmother had died when he was much younger, he knew she, too, would approve of Lauren's effort to make a home out of their neglected old homestead. Lauren smiled at the compliment as if she'd just been awarded a blue ribbon, and Travis felt something unfamiliar take a hold of his heart. She looked so pretty and so very pleased with his reaction that he had to shove his hands in his pockets to keep from putting them all over her.

"Come on," she urged, deliberately tugging one of his hands out of safekeeping. "Let me show you the rest of the place."

Her fingers laced through his. A hot rush of awareness ran the length of Travis's arm and tightened his groin. A wiser man would have made up some excuse to leave—like the sudden need to take an ice-cold shower. Swinging the bathroom door open, Lauren offered him the opportunity to do so. She presented him with a view of a familiar antique claw foot tub, all shined up and newly fitted with a hand-held showerhead. Candles, bubble bath and soft towels rested on a small wooden table alongside a modest collection of cosmetics. Three coordinated pictures of flowers hung in a line above the tub, and a full-length mirror placed strategically in front of a white woven bath mat brought to mind erotic images of a dripping wet Lauren stepping from the tub to dry herself in duplicate—the real her and the reflection of her.

There was no need to run any hot water from the tap to steam up Travis's mental mirror.

"Nice," he croaked, hoping she would assume he was referring to the room and not all the wicked things he imagined doing to her with that showerhead.

"Come on," she urged.

Since the cabin consisted of only three rooms and a porch, that left just the bedroom for his perusal. Travis swallowed. If it had been hard not picturing Lauren naked in the bathroom, it was downright impossible not to imagine her sprawled out in all her womanly glory upon the soft pink bedspread that accessorized a headboard with roses painted on its porcelain knobs. Normally Travis would have felt out of place in such a feminine room, but somehow Lauren's bedroom was just as inviting as the rest of the house.

If not more so.

Positioning herself on the edge of the bed, she looked up at him with such a sweet, albeit tipsy, expression that he wasn't sure he could meet the challenge of leaving before he initiated something that they would both later regret.

Lauren shot him a rueful smile. "I never thought I'd see the day when I'd be entertaining Travis Banks in my bedroom."

"Why not?"

"Why not?" she parroted with a squeak that emphasized her own sense of disbelief. "Need I remind you that when you were a senior in high school, you couldn't so much as be bothered to give a little nobody freshman like me the time of day?"

Travis put a pucker between his eyebrows as if he were taxing his memory. "I don't recall you ever asking me for it."

"I didn't have the nerve," Lauren admitted.

Travis sighed. If he'd somehow hurt her feelings back then, it was certainly not intentional on his part.

"Actually, I don't remember a lot about my senior year other than how hard it was trying to fit my athletic schedule around chores at home and worrying about my grandpa who was dying of cancer. But, now that you mention it, I do vaguely recall you just about melting into the floor the few times I tried to so much as make eye contact with you."

Lauren felt the blood creep up her neck. It was hard enough getting her fuzzy thoughts around the fact that

Travis remembered her at all, let alone entertaining the idea that her hero's feet actually touched the ground those many years ago. Back then it had never occurred to her that he might be struggling with anything more important than how to juggle cheerleaders and footballs at the same time. Lauren could tell by the way Travis's voice softened every time he mentioned his grandfather that they had shared a close bond. Not unlike the one she shared with the father she had lost about the same time.

"I'm afraid you still have the same effect on me," she confessed, referring to his remark about her melting away at the sight of him.

"You have a different effect on me now."

Travis's voice was deep and throaty and laden with palpable implications. That acknowledgment was enough to send Lauren's already woozy sense of equilibrium into loop-to-loops. When she'd hid her secret crush behind a pile of schoolbooks, her adolescent brain could not have invented a more delicious scene than the one unfolding right now. Having gone to a great deal of trouble to put herself out there tonight, Lauren thought that it would be a shame to simply turn out the light on this evening without reexamining her old fantasies and indulging her curiosity at long last. Travis may not be the marrying type, but that wasn't to say he wasn't attracted to her. Or her to him.

From the very first time she'd seen it, Lauren had loved his face. The clean, fresh-scrubbed, all-American look of it. The humor and vision shining from those mercurial gray eyes of his. And the cockeyed, boyish smile that could get him out of trouble in any teacher's class.

Especially hers.

Time had done nothing to diminish Lauren's feelings for him. It had, in fact, only intensified them.

That he was looking at her as if he wanted to eat her alive emboldened her. Having worked up a good appetite herself, she couldn't bring herself to turn away from such a sumptuous banquet. Just because this was a once in a lifetime feast, didn't mean she should refrain from sampling the gourmet menu out of fear of ruining her taste for more ordinary fare.

Lauren forced herself not to melt when she made eye contact this time. Anticipation zinged through her like a jolt of pure electricity. The look Travis gave her in return was hot enough to cause spontaneous combustion. She doubted the portable extinguisher she kept under the sink would have the least effect upon the fire they were about to start.

"How about you tuck me in tonight?" she asked over the thunderous beating of her heart.

His voice sounded like it was being dragged over broken glass. "I don't think that's such a good idea."

Ignoring that counsel, she kicked off her high heels and lay back against the pillows, hoping to strike a seductive pose. Catching her reflection in the mirror above her dresser, she thought she looked pretty darn good, too, even though she felt somewhat ridiculous.

"I think it's a great idea."

"You've had too much to drink, Lauren. A gentleman doesn't take advantage of a lady under those circumstances."

Travis's rumbling voice echoed off the walls and reverberated inside Lauren's bones. Taking his gallantry as a personal rebuff, she recalled whispered conversations implying that he wasn't always so chivalrous.

Apparently he just didn't want *her.*

Lauren wondered what circumstances might provoke him to abandon such unexpected principles. The thought challenged a womanly sense of defiance buried deep inside her. A coy smile toyed with the edges of her mouth.

"Who says I want you to be gentleman tonight? Rumor has it you're not always so gallant."

A muscle along his jawline jumped, and his gray eyes darkened to the color of gathering storm clouds. His voice was deep in his throat.

"Then I doubt you've been talking to any real ladies."

"Maybe not," Lauren agreed easily enough. She reached down to unbuckle her belt. "And maybe what you've heard about what kind of a lady I am has been exaggerated as well."

Travis's laughter boomed in the small room, wounding her. Clearly he wasn't buying her femme fatale act. She sat up on the edge of the bed and confronted him with the boring facts of her life.

"Okay, maybe I'm no swinging single, but let me tell you being a lady isn't all it's cracked up to be.

A note of wistfulness crept into her voice as she continued.

"Being on best behavior all the time has done little but leave me lonely. Don't you want to be the one to unmask a terminally good girl and set her free at last?"

The look of amusement on Travis's handsome face vanished. Desire took its place, but restraint made its presence known as well.

"Are you sure that's what you want?" he asked flatly.

Lauren's throat went tight and her heart seemed to be pounding to get out.

"Positive."

One hundred percent.

She'd never been more certain of anything in her life. She was tired of living life from the outside looking in. Tired of tamping down her own desires just because some pesky little voice in her head refused to let her take a risk. Lauren knew it was hopeless to think anything permanent would come out of this act of rebellion, of pure self-indulgence.

But that didn't make her want Travis any less.

"Have it your way then. Just don't go expecting more than I can give you afterward."

Though his words were far from romantic, the sound of his zipper sliding down was the most erotic thing Lauren had ever heard. She held her breath. Nothing could have torn her gaze away from the sight of Travis stripping for her. Sandy hair dusted a well-muscled chest, trailed down a washboard stomach and disappeared beneath the waistband of a pair of jeans hanging precariously low on a pair of masculine hips. He tossed his shirt upon on the floor and was tugging his boots off before it occurred to him to ask one very crucial question.

"You are on birth control, aren't you?"

Cursing herself for her lack of foresight, Lauren focused her gaze on his bare chest and mutely shook her head. Any fantasies she might have had about him being the one who wanted children in his previous marriage dissolved on the spot.

Travis swore under his breath.

Lauren supposed he had a right to be angry. As adamant as he was about preserving his bachelor status, he certainly didn't need a baby complicating his life. Hers either, for that matter—at least until she met a settling-down kind of man who wanted children as much as she did. That didn't lessen the sense of disappointment that swamped her at the thought that this night may well be over before it even began however.

"Don't you carry something with you?" she asked meekly.

Travis glared at her. "I don't know what you've heard about me, but for your information, I'm not a walking drugstore and I don't sleep around indiscriminately."

Lauren was glad the local gossips had it wrong. Not that it helped do anything to solve her present predicament: that of wanting this man more than life itself and being in the position to do nothing about it. She doubted whether she'd ever be able to muster up the courage to throw herself at him again.

"Maybe we should just forget the whole thing," Travis suggested in a tone that sounded less than chivalrous as he ran a hand through his hair in a gesture of pure frustration.

"Maybe I don't want to."

The petulance in her own voice surprised Lauren. She hadn't waited this long and worked herself into such a state to let opportunity pass her by so easily. All of a sudden she didn't care if she sounded forward. She didn't even care if she sounded desperate.

The last time she'd had sex she'd been too inexperienced and nervous to truly enjoy the experience. Tonight was going to be different. Tonight would fulfill the fantasies of a girl who'd never allowed herself to do more than dream of Travis Banks between the sheets of her lonely twin bed.

"Don't you have something at home?" she asked. "For emergencies."

The hard, searching look that Travis gave her left her feeling weightless.

"We're not at my house. If you really want to do this, I suppose I could run over there and check, but you have to promise not to pass out in the meantime."

As if she could possibly fall asleep! The chances of that happening were as likely as Travis reappearing with a wedding ring instead of a prophylactic. Worried that she was risking the humiliation of waiting naked for him when he had no intention of coming back, Lauren asked for the bare minimum in terms of commitments from him.

"I'll promise—if in return, you'll promise not to get lost on the way."

Travis's expression turned feral, and his voice lowered to a growl.

"Don't even think about falling asleep. I'll be right back."

With that, he disappeared into the night, leaving Lauren feeling as powerful as a magician. And as helpless as a bunny plucked from a black top hat by the swish of a wand.

Travis hadn't bothered putting on his shirt. Lauren hoped the cold air on his bare skin would motivate him to hurry, although if he was anywhere near as hot as she at the moment, nothing short of fulfillment was likely to have any effect on his temperature. However the second that she heard the front door close behind Travis, her bravado deserted her. Her mind raced with unanswered questions that immobilized her with fear.

What if I can't please him?

What if sex ruins our relationship, and I end up losing the only nice affordable rental in the county?

And what does one wear to a full-fledged seduction?

Never having bothered to replace the old nightgown she'd given to Goodwill, Lauren had simply been sleeping in the nude since moving out of her mother's house. As tempted as she was to slip into an oversize T-shirt, pull the covers up to her chin and make herself invisible again before Travis could get back, she had no intention of letting him know just how nervous she really was.

Now was not the time for belated caution.

Now was the time to go all out and make her dreams come true—if only for this one very special night.

Six

Stumbling through sagebrush and clumps of cactus in the dark, Travis cursed his weakness as a man. It bothered him that Lauren considered him some kind of playboy. Especially since nothing could be farther from the truth.

Oh, he'd be the first to admit that he was no saint. He wasn't cut out for a lifetime of celibacy, but that didn't mean he'd bed down with any woman who gave him the slightest encouragement. In fact, he hoped the ancient condoms he kept stashed away in the back corner of his underwear drawer hadn't outlived their shelf life.

With the notable exception of Lauren, all the women he'd been with since his divorce all claimed to be on birth control. They had been quick to assure him they were looking for nothing more than a good time.

If any of them had a change of heart after getting to know him better, Travis promptly replayed his standard message about not being interested in long-term relationships.

He couldn't help it if that earned him a reputation around town as a cold bastard.

He'd learned the hard way that it was far better to err on the side of honesty than to marry someone just because it might make *her* happy. As hard as he'd tried to make his marriage work, there wasn't a man alive who could make Jaclyn content. Every time he signed another outrageous alimony check, he counted himself lucky to have gotten out of the relationship relatively unscathed. Until he saw someone going gaga over a baby and the weight of his loss crushed the air from his lungs.

That somber reminder did little to cool the desire throbbing through his veins, a testimony to the power Lauren held over him. Sharper than cactus barbs, the sting of conscience urged him to stop this insanity before someone got hurt. He assured himself that she knew exactly where things stood between them. Hadn't he been completely up front with her from the outset?

Besides, just because Lauren was ready to make love to him didn't mean she would be expecting an engagement ring in the morning. He was probably just being paranoid. She certainly hadn't made any noise in that direction so there was no reason to expect that she would.

At least that's what he told himself over and over again as he marched toward her cabin beneath the full moon, all the while clutching a handful of condoms as if he were holding the Holy Grail.

Disheveled and sexy as hell, Travis looked as though he had run the short distance in record time. The effort had done nothing to lessen the yearning shining in his eyes. That predatory look made Lauren tremble from the inside out. Opening his hand, he held out a small cellophane packet.

He sounded out of breath as he gave Lauren yet another chance to back out. "If you've changed your mind, now would be a real good time to tell me."

Having no idea how many condoms came in a pack, Lauren hoped her voice wouldn't betray her ignorance. She feigned a wicked smile and patted the pillow next to her.

"I just hope you brought enough."

Travis's laugh rumbled out of a place deep in his chest as he pulled her off the bed and onto her feet. "And how many do you think I'll need to satisfy you?"

Lauren had no idea. Barely managing to pull off her shoes and nylons and belt in the time he was gone, she was happy to leave the remainder of her undressing in his capable hands—especially considering that her own hands were none too steady. Travis reached around her to undo the zipper running down the back of her dress. It fell open revealing the curve of her back. She shivered.

But not from the cold.

When he pushed the fabric off her shoulders, it was all Lauren could do to refrain from catching the dress as it slipped over her breasts and pooled at her feet. Travis wasted no time in disposing of her nearly translucent slip. She stepped out of the pile of clothing at her feet to stand before him in a lacy bra and matching wisp of panties.

Lauren felt exposed as a fraud. Not nearly as comfortable with herself as she pretended to be, she expected him to find fault with her body. She was nowhere near as thin as the models who sold such fantasy wear in the magazines. And a good deal older.

Travis didn't seem to mind. His eyes trailed hungrily down the length of her body and back up again, resting on the swell of breasts spilling over a ridiculously skimpy bra that she'd bought on impulse in anticipation of just such a moment. His hands were hot as he tested the fullness of each breast, cupping each one gently before bending down to place a kiss between them. A surge of heat swept through Lauren. Her knees wobbled. Swaying, she threw her head back, gasped for breath and dug her nails into the flesh of his shoulders.

He didn't complain. Standing to his full height, he drew her flush against him and encircled her in his arms. So nimbly did he undo the clasp of her bra that she didn't even realize it until the lace fell from her shoulders to encircle her wrists. Taking one hard nipple into his mouth, he suckled gently as she tried to rid herself of her shackles.

Travis didn't seem the least interested in helping her escape.

Desperate mewling sounds came from some place

deep inside Lauren. She could no more stop them than she could stem the waters of a raging river overflowing its banks. When Travis drew away at last, she offered him the tip of the other breast, swollen equally with wanting.

"Good girl," he murmured, his voice soft and seductive.

The next thing Lauren knew, she was flat on her back in bed and he was pulling off her panties. With his teeth. Never having thought of herself as a screamer, she was suddenly glad that they were miles away from the nearest house. The noises welling up inside her could not be contained as his teeth scraped the gentle flesh along her inner thigh and his tongue teased its way all down the length of her legs.

Wrapped up in the most exquisite sensations she'd ever imagined, Lauren watched with undivided concentration as he raised himself up and proceeded to strip for her. She was thankful the process didn't take long because she didn't think she could stand waiting much longer before begging him to hurry. Already shirtless, his upper body was exposed by the moonlight spilling through the window. He was a perfect sculpture cast in silver.

Travis divested himself of his boots and jeans. A pair of plain white boxer shorts tented out in an obvious display of arousal that was fully exposed a second later when he tossed them among the growing pile of clothing on the floor. He unwrapped the foil package and sheathed himself. All muscle and sinew and perfect masculine strength, he took Lauren's breath away.

"You're so beautiful."

That those words came from Travis's mouth and not her own took Lauren by surprise. She allowed the compliment to seep into her heart. Whether she was lacking physically in comparison to others wasn't the issue. She *felt* beautiful. Desirable. Deliberately shutting off the schoolteacher part of her brain that caused her to over-analyze just about everything, she freed herself of thought and gave herself over to the pure rapture of the moment.

Never in her wildest dreams had she imagined Travis to be such an amazing lover—and she was a woman who prided herself on her imagination. Having been disappointed in the past, Lauren reveled in the eroticism of being with a man who truly knew how to pleasure a woman. Lowering himself over her, Travis pressed the length of himself against her belly and branded her with the knowledge that she was about to be filled completely. She was immediately seized by the worry that she would not be able to accommodate his considerable size.

The instant his lips touched hers, however, that anxiety disappeared and was replaced by the most heavenly sensation. Long, liquid kisses carried her away as Travis prodded the seam of her lips with the tip of his tongue. When Lauren had dreamed about having sex with Travis, she had neglected to include the tenderness of his kisses.

Kisses as demanding as they were soul searching.

Moaning, Lauren parted her lips for him, and Travis thrust his tongue inside. Writhing with pleasure, Lauren placed her hands on either side of his neck and held him close. Without breaking their kiss, she wrapped her legs around him and splayed her fingers through his hair. Never had she felt more completely connected with another human being.

Feeling suddenly brave, Lauren reached down and took his shaft into one hand.

"Squeeze," he commanded in a hoarse whisper.

Good girl that she was, Lauren did as she was told. He was hard and hot. And vulnerable. It gave her the most incredible sense of power to hold this man in the palm of her hand. And it filled her with an overwhelming sense of love for him.

Love?

The word materialized in her consciousness like lightning striking the center of a dark forest. Only she could see the blinding flash, the glowing spark that was struck. Lauren knew it was capable of razing everything in its path.

Including herself.

She told herself that she was a silly fool to fall head over heels in love with a man so committed to his single life.

Then she heard herself scream, and rational thought dissolved into nothingness. It was not a scream of fright or of pain, but rather a primal reaction to Travis pressing the tip of his shaft against her clitoris. Lauren arched her back. She dug her fingernails into the hard plane of his back and unleashed the animal deep inside her.

"I don't," Travis gasped, holding back, "want to hurt you."

"You won't," Lauren lied.

The body knows things long before the mind can accept them. Physical pain was not a priority at the moment. Nor was the certainty that she was destined to pay an emotional price later. Seeking the exquisite perfection of her love for this man, Lauren knew only that her soul would tear apart at the seams if he did not complete what he had started.

Travis plunged deep inside her with an urgency that seemed to surprise even him. Nothing in Lauren's life had prepared her for the utter bliss of being filled so completely by such a man. Of surrounding him with her warm, willing flesh. Of simply letting go. And letting herself go a little crazy.

Moving her body in unison with his, Lauren met him stroke for furious stroke. She climaxed quickly. Clawing and gasping and forgetting her own name, she called his out as if it were a magical incantation. The sensations assaulting her from every direction were sublime. Her body clenched in spasms of white-hot flame, demanding that Travis succumb to his own need. The muscles of his neck corded as he closed his eyes and threw his head back. Buried to the hilt, he exploded.

Lauren filled her senses with that glorious sight, holding him deep inside her until well after the throbbing subsided. Panting and slick with sweat, Travis opened his eyes to regard her with wonder. She smiled at him almost shyly and spiraled back to earth in his arms. Although she did not want to let go of what she was feeling for this man, she was also afraid of holding on too tight.

Was after-play too much to expect after such an incredible experience?

She brushed a damp lock of hair away from Travis's forehead. With infinite tenderness she traced an eyebrow with the tip of her index finger, stroked the stubble of a cheek that would need to see a razor in the morning and raised her head up to suckle the lobe of his ear.

"That was very nice," she murmured.

Travis blanched at the tepid choice of words.

"Nice?"

"Fabulous," Lauren amended.

In fact, she hadn't believed it possible for earthbound creatures to experience such ecstasy in this life. Although words could not do it justice, she did her best.

"Spectacular. Fantastic. Incredible. Mind-bending. Life-altering. Utterly indescribable."

"That's better," Travis growled.

He wrapped his warm body around her as if to say he wasn't letting go anytime soon. Lauren didn't want to go anywhere else. Pressing an ear to his chest, she listened to the life song beating there in steady cadence. A woman in love, she heard the echo of her own spirit. And though she knew better than to blurt out such a raw, untested proclamation so soon, Lauren refused to think about the consequences of giving her heart to a man who wasn't ready to accept it.

For once in her life, she wasn't going to let herself think about the future and all its complications. Not when the present was so perfect.

And so damned fleeting.

Seven

A pink sun climbed behind a bank of clouds to spill dawn upon a glorious new day. Filtered through lace curtains, the morning light tattooed dancing patterns on Lauren's shoulder and that of the man sleeping so soundly next to her. She stretched her hand out to the sunbeam, marveling that it hadn't turned her invisible again.

Or made Travis disappear.

Lauren was certain that heaven would have difficulty competing with the feeling of waking in his strong arms, sharing his body warmth and savoring the sweet soreness of being so thoroughly loved. While he slept, she studied him at length. Time had honed the boyish good looks she had loved so well and turned Travis into a man slightly too rugged for the cover of slick fashion magazines. The stubble along his jawline lent roughness to the peaceful expression that he wore while sleeping. Lauren couldn't resist finger-combing his short blond hair. Natural highlights caught the sunshine and warmed each strand to the touch.

Oh, what she would give to start out each day appreciating this man's finer attributes! Those on the inside as well as the outside. He had his quirks. That much was true. Who didn't? Scarred by the past, Travis was clearly afraid to let his guard down. But Lauren knew him as a good man. The fact that he was willing to rush in to a save a damsel in distress—whether she wanted to be rescued or not—was testimony to his own personal sense of integrity. And despite her assertion that she could take care of herself just fine, thank you very much, she secretly longed to renew her faith in long forgotten fantasies about knights on white horses.

Lauren understood that Travis didn't feel the same way about her that she did about him, but she couldn't believe that passion such as theirs could be born in the absence of emotion, either. Watching his chest rise and fall in steady rhythm, she couldn't help but wonder what it would be like to have his children. She fantasized briefly about standing over a crib and gazing upon the sleeping angel such a union was sure to produce. Would the baby be as beautiful as his father? As inquisitive as her mother?

Something sweet and unbidden welled up in Lauren's heart, and moisture rose unexpectedly to her eyes.

Stop it! she told herself fiercely.

Such dreams could only lead to heartbreak and ruin the perfection of the moment. She refused to let concerns about the future drain the joy out of the present. For the precious time being, the man of her dreams belonged to her.

At least until he woke up.

Impulse drew her hand over his heart. Cupping it like she would to protect a flame from the wind, Lauren said a prayer over its steady rhythm.

"Good morning, gorgeous."

The sound of that voice, gravelly with the first utterance of the day, startled Lauren so that she drew her hand back as if caught in the act of stealing. She savored the sound of that tender endearment on his lips. However, without benefit of a comb or makeup or toothbrush, it was hard for her to believe its reliability.

"Good morning," she repeated.

Eyes the color of lifting fog reassured her. And beheld her gently. She was relieved to see that Travis gave no sign of bolting from bed once awareness of his surroundings settled over him. Instead he drew her close and asked for a kiss.

Lauren clamped her mouth shut. "Sorry—morning breath," she mumbled apologetically.

A spark of irritation flashed over Travis's face.

"Kiss me," he demanded over the rumbling of his empty stomach.

Lauren succumbed, doing as she was told and giving herself over to a man who, by the feel of things, had something other than breakfast on his mind. Relatively inexperienced in such matters, she was pleasantly surprised to discover that he awoke in a state of arousal. A firm squeeze was all the invitation Travis needed to start the day out right. Dragging her on top of him, he gave her permission to forget all about her morning breath.

Lauren's laughter was deep and full as she sat up and reached for the only remaining cellophane packet left on her nightstand.

"You'll have to replenish your supply," Lauren chastised, struggling to open a package designed to deter less determined lovers. "And I'll have to figure out how to work these things myself."

Travis grinned as he watched her take a corner between her teeth and rip it open. Positioning himself to make the rest of the task as easy as possible, he clasped his hands behind his head and, with a satisfied sigh, offered to help in any way he could.

"I'd rather do it myself," Lauren said assuming the masterful tone of a dominatrix in training.

Putting a little elastic covering over such an impressive erection proved a lot harder than Travis had made it look last night. When the condom shot out of Lauren's hands like a rubber band that some rowdy student might try launching when her back was turned to the class, she burst into a fit of giggles that would have made a less secure man shrivel up. Travis's patience was rivaled only by the tenacity of his libido.

He rolled his eyes good-naturedly and retrieved the condom from where it landed next to his pillow.

"I thought teachers were supposed to do it with class."

"Just with an eye to perfection. And if that means having to stay after class to bring up your grade, you just might find yourself assigned to permanent detention, mister."

Travis didn't complain about such harsh punishment. In fact, he seemed determined to teach her a thing or two. An amazing lover, he was both gentle and demanding in turn. He caressed, kneaded, suckled and rubbed her all the right ways and in all the right places. Ignoring her pleas that she couldn't possibly come again, he made sure she climaxed several times before allowing himself the same satisfaction.

The intensity of his expression as his body strained for the paroxysm of release was so stirring that Lauren deliberately imprinted the sight in her mind. Though she longed for a lifetime of such sublime moments, she was afraid it would be an image that would have to last her forever. Indeed, Travis had issued warnings in place of promises regarding the future.

Spent so early in the day, they lay intertwined in each other's arms, soaking up the morning sun and enjoying each other's company. Such mind-boggling sex could become addictive, Lauren thought as she finally dragged herself out of bed to face the day a new woman.

Having never showered with a man before, she was reluctant to do so now. Considering the time they had just spent together, it seemed silly to defer to modesty. Besides, how could she argue with Travis's assurance that "a little clean fun never hurt anyone"?

Beneath a stream of warm water, Lauren savored

the tender ministries paid to her body after such intense lovemaking. Travis lathered her up from chin to toe with soap and gently ran a clean washcloth over all her curves, making sure no trace remained on any part of her body before turning his attention to her hair. She purred with pleasure as he rubbed shampoo into her hair and massaged her scalp with expert fingers. Tipping her head back, she let the water rinse away her troubles. The next thing she knew, Travis had her pinned against the shower wall and was kissing her all over.

Clinging to his slick body, Lauren discovered he was rock-hard again. And had to apologize for being too sore to indulge him so soon after their sex marathon.

"No problem," he assured her, kneeling down before her and nudging her legs apart.

A mouthful of water and a hot surge of pleasure prevented Lauren from protesting. Pressing her spine against the wall, she braced herself against the onslaught of ecstasy. The tip of his tongue settled on a highly sensitive spot, and she tried to keep from drowning in the sensations flowing through her. If she could have managed to form the words, she might have begged him to stop.

To never stop...

Just when Lauren thought she couldn't stand another second of such exquisite torture, her body folded around itself from the inside out and burst into spasmodic contractions that left her too weak to stand up. The running water did little to muffle the sounds of whimpering that echoed through the cabin. Travis looked thoroughly pleased by the fact that he had to hold her up to keep her from slipping down the drain.

Once Lauren's bones were restored to their proper state, she took it upon herself to fix a hearty breakfast for the man who had so thoroughly satisfied her. A good cook, she liked to keep a full pantry. Wearing nothing but blue jeans, Travis sat at her cozy kitchen table drinking coffee and looking as though he belonged there. As the smell of bacon and pancakes wafted through the kitchen, Lauren was filled with a sense of contentment unlike any she had ever known before.

Ravenous, Travis piled his plate high with the food she set on the table in front of him. A large pat of butter melted down the sides of a stack of steaming hotcakes. Lauren didn't skimp on the warm syrup pooling around the edifice like a moat, either. He'd devoured half a dozen pieces of bacon before the pancakes even reached the table. If his sighs of satisfaction were any indication, the old adage that the way to a man's heart was through his stomach was right on target.

"Very nice," Travis said.

There was a hint of surprise in the statement as if he were setting a new precedent in sticking around for breakfast after a night of incredibly hot sex. Hoping he might linger longer, Lauren poured him another cup of coffee. She tucked into her memory banks that he liked it strong and black. He smiled over the rim of his cup.

Her little kitchen seemed even cozier with him in it. The hum of the refrigerator in the background went unnoticed. Still damp from the shower they had shared, Travis's hair was a shade darker when wet. Lauren noticed that a farmer's tan bisected muscles defined by hard work and that his arms bore the scars of his labor. In all her fantasies about this man, no one had included such a mundane yet poignant scene as what they shared over the smell of chicory and bacon.

"I don't suppose you could take the rest of the day off to spend with me," she asked in a small, hopeful voice.

The fork poised halfway to Travis's sensual mouth stopped. Watching him fumble for words—for any excuse to make a quick getaway—made Lauren painfully aware of her mistake. She shouldn't have pressed for anything that smacked of a continued relationship—and certainly for nothing that would hint of their romance in public. A wave of indignation swept over her.

Travis swallowed hard as if the last bite of his food was stuck in his throat.

"I've got an awful lot to do today," he said at last.

Lauren shrugged her shoulders with an indifference she did not feel. It hadn't been her intention to push him away. She hadn't thought he would be so frightened by the prospect of spending time with her outside the bedroom. She held up a hand to stop him in the middle of listing off the day's obligations.

"You don't owe me any explanations."

He really didn't. It wasn't like they had any kind of understanding beyond their undeniable physical attraction for one another. She knew the score.

Why then, Lauren wondered, did she have such an irresistible urge to pour the last of the syrup over his head?

Seeming suddenly as awkward as a handful of thumbs, Travis let his fork clatter against his plate. He pushed his empty plate away and put his hands against the edge of the table.

"Here, let me help you clear the table before I go," he offered.

"No thanks."

Lauren began gathering up the rest of the dirty dishes. She'd be damned if she let him see how badly she'd been hurt by his reaction to such a harmless request. It wasn't as if she'd proposed to him or anything nearly so horrifying.

"When I don't have so much going on, I'll take the day off and we can go do something fun, " Travis offered lamely.

Lauren remained aloof. Had the offer not been born out of guilt and a desire to pacify her, she might have been moved to give him more than a tight little smile and a noncommittal, "Maybe."

Travis ground a heel into the braided rug beneath his feet as if he were settling himself into the starting blocks of a long-distance race.

"What's wrong?" he asked.

"Nothing."

Lauren took perverse pleasure in the fact that Travis looked so very put out with her single word responses to the questions he posed.

"Look," he said with an air of exasperation. "I never made you any promises. If you'll recall, I was the one who thought this might be a bad idea in the first place. Just because we spent the night together doesn't automatically equate to a long-term commitment."

The man's arrogance was as infuriating as his morning-after breakups were legendary. Refusing to give him the satisfaction of knowing just how much it hurt to be tossed aside in such a cavalier manner, Lauren summoned a soft, calm tone that only those who knew her very well might recognize as a sign of mounting fury.

"It certainly doesn't," she replied. "And since you're being so brutally honest, I'd like to take the opportunity to set the record straight myself."

Ignoring the defensive posture her warning evoked from him, Lauren continued evenly. "Last night was wonderful. I'll cherish the memory forever. But I hope you're not expecting some kind of formal thank-you from me. Just because you slept with me once doesn't equate to an open invitation to spend the night whenever you feel like it, either."

She was reminded of a fish studying a bare hook as Travis's lower jaw swung open. Not inclined to bait that hook for him, she stood her ground with as much dignity as she could muster under the circumstances.

"You've made it perfectly clear that you aren't looking for a commitment. I've been just as up front about the fact that I am. You don't have to worry about hurting my feelings. I'm a big girl, and I knew what I was getting into. One night certainly doesn't a lifetime make, so why don't we just part as friends and leave it at that?"

* * *

Travis wouldn't have been surprised had Lauren stuck out her hand and asked him to shake on it. He couldn't remember ever being so politely kicked to the gutter before. This conversation gave him a whole new empathy for those poor women who had harangued him on his answering machine after he broke it off with them. For a man who'd been so eager to hit the front door running just a moment ago, he was suddenly reluctant to put one foot in front of the other and make a graceful exit.

"Friends it is then," he mumbled, aware that he was being neither sincere nor enthusiastic as a little voice in his head pressed to know why after such mind-boggling sex they were parting at all.

Because you have such a busy day ahead of you, remember, idiot? Because that love 'em and leave 'em attitude of yours doesn't apply to a woman like this one who deserves more than you're willing to give. Because you're afraid of getting hurt and don't ever want to go through another messy divorce.

Travis met Lauren's gaze over the proud tilt of her chin and accepted the tight smile she gave him before turning her back to him. He walked into the bedroom to finish dressing before leaving. He doubted she even heard the door close behind him over the sound of dishes rattling and water running in the sink.

Ambling back to his own house, he wondered why he was so unhappy about getting exactly what he'd asked for. Last night's no-strings-attached sex had been fantastic, but he wasn't looking for a long-term relationship. He definitely didn't want to get married. He liked the freedom the single life gave him.

But he didn't want Lauren seeing anyone else....

The thought of her returning to The Alibi without him made him grow hot and prickly all over.

In short, he was the proverbial dog in the manger. Finding the analogy unflattering, Travis grabbed a pair of worn leather gloves and set to working Lauren out of his system the only way he could think of that didn't involve a bottle of whiskey. Experience had taught him that hard physical labor was an amazing panacea.

Just put her out of your mind, he repeated to himself over and over again.

That particular mantra was easier said than done. Hoisting bales of hay into the back of his pickup a short while later, Travis was assailed by unbidden visions of Lauren half-naked. Of Lauren completely naked. Of Lauren struggling to open a cellophane condom wrapper with her teeth. Of Lauren struggling to take all of him.

Lauren innocent.

Lauren glorious in her discovery of how to thoroughly please a man—and herself.

A mixture of startling contrasts, the woman played with Travis's mind long past the point where his muscles and a seemingly insurmountable list of chores gave out. For dinner he substituted a stiff drink for the steak that he couldn't get past the lump in his throat. Settling himself in front of the television set for a night of marathon ESPN, he gazed across the short distance separating their homes and caught a glimpse of Lauren's silhouette against a pair of lacy curtains as she prepared for bed.

His mouth went dry. Not a voyeur by nature, Travis could no more turn aside from that mesmerizing sight than he'd been able to force his thoughts away from Lauren all day long. She pulled her shirt over her head to expose the lacy froth of a bra supporting a pair of breasts that he now knew fit his large hands perfectly. Putting her hands to the back of her neck, she stretched and leisurely arched her back in the way that cats do to make themselves comfortable before a nap.

Reaching behind herself to undo the clasp, she presented a profile that caused all the blood in Travis's body to pool in his loins at once. Lauren proceeded to divest herself of her bra and shorts and matching panties before picking up a bottle of scented lotion from her bed stand and slathering it all over herself. Travis was familiar with that alluring honeysuckle fragrance since he had rubbed it all over her skin less than twenty-four hours ago.

The moan he heard was his own.

Disappearing from the window frame, Lauren shut the light off, oblivious to what she was doing to him. Travis ached with longing. He scolded himself for being so weak. Determined not to let testosterone do his thinking for him, he faced his empty bed with grim determination.

And spent the rest of the night fighting demons of his own damned making.

Eight

"**A**ny harm in a *friend* offering to lend a helping hand?"

The familiar husky voice behind Lauren almost knocked her off the stool on which she was so precariously perched. Clearly, Travis's deliberate choice of words was a reference to the way she'd left things between them yesterday. Wavering between wanting to tell him to go to hell and gratitude for his unexpected help, she struggled to maintain her footing.

Literally and figuratively.

Lauren's muscles ached, and her heart followed suit.

"I'd appreciate it," she admitted, letting the screwdriver she'd been holding in her mouth fall to the ground.

Lauren didn't know that Travis had been watching

her struggle to put up the wooden swing for the past fifteen minutes before appearing oh so nonchalantly on her porch. Only aware of how clumsy and scruffy she must look, she wished she'd put on something sexier than a pair of old cutoffs and a T-shirt before tackling what had, at the outset, appeared to be a fairly simple job.

"Here, let me help you down," Travis offered, putting his hands on either side of her hips in an effort to steady her.

It had the opposite effect. Swaying, Lauren reached for a pair of shoulders as sturdy as twin boulders only to see herself reflected in his smoldering eyes. She railed against the image of the fainting heroine in dated love stories.

Don't you dare swoon!

After a night spent tossing and turning, she thought he looked far too rested. Travis carried her the short distance to the porch railing where he proceeded to let her down slowly. So slowly in fact that she couldn't help but notice every bulging muscle as she slid down the hard planes of his front. Lauren resisted the urge to rub up against him the way instinct begged her to.

"You look good," he said, setting her upon the porch railing.

Goose bumps appeared on her arms.

"It's a look I like to call chic grunge."

In the heat of the midday sun, Lauren shivered violently. So absorbed was she in her reaction to Travis's close proximity that it took her a moment to realize that her butt was squarely on the porch railing and there was no longer any need to cling to him for support. And she was embarrassed to discover that her legs were open wide to accommodate his body's placement.

Would he accept nothing less than her complete humiliation?

Breathing in shallow gasps, she let her hands slip to his well-defined pectoral muscles. And pushed him away. Hard. Travis stepped back with a surprised look upon his face, giving her the opportunity to clamp her legs shut. The fact that she was throbbing with desire wasn't something she wanted him to know. Striving for an aloofness that she did not feel, Lauren attempted to strike a pose somewhere between Mae West and a buddy.

"Thanks."

She hopped off the railing only to find herself trapped between Travis and a piece of knotty pine. Leaning in, he placed one hand on the post and dropped the other to the small of her back. He breathed in the scent of her signature perfume and sighed in exaggeration.

"And you smell good, too."

Waves of heat supplanted the shivers that had beleaguered Lauren a moment ago.

Hot and cold.

Just like Travis himself.

A scorching smack of resentment had her spouting the same lame excuse he'd used yesterday to avoid spending time with her.

"I'd invite you in for dinner after you finish hanging my swing, but I'm sure you've got lots of work to do, and I wouldn't want to get in your way."

"It just so happens I have some free time on my hands today. And I'm famished," Travis assured her with a flash of white teeth that reminded Lauren of childhood images of the big bad wolf.

The gleam in his eyes left no doubt what he was hungry for.

A convenient snack, not an entire meal...

"Sorry. Unfortunately, *I* happen to have plans later today."

Something stronger than mere curiosity flashed across the cloudy skies of Travis's eyes.

"Like what?" he asked.

Lauren thought about telling him that she had a date just to see his reaction. Not the kind of woman who was into playing mind games however, she decided to keep her tone friendly and her words matter-of-fact. She figured the last thing Travis would want to do was to accompany her to a family function—one in which her relatives would immediately leap to all kinds of assumptions about the two of them if they showed up together. And ask all sorts of embarrassing questions that she'd just as soon avoid.

"Like something that doesn't involve you, but I'd be glad to fix you a sandwich for your trouble before I take off."

Letting go of the post, Travis put both hands around her back and bent her slightly over the railing.

"I don't remember mentioning food when I said I was famished," he clarified for her benefit.

His lips found the sweet hollow of her neck. Clean-shaven, he nuzzled her. A delicious shiver ran through Lauren, and she felt herself falling over backward under the weight of his charm. With deliberate expertise, Travis trailed kisses up the curve of her neck. When he at last reached her earlobe, he took a delicate nibble.

"Yum, yum."

Lauren hated herself for the whimper that escaped her lips. It took every ounce of self-control she had left to turn aside when he lowered his mouth to hers. His lips grazed her cheek.

"Stop it!"

She was tempted to slap the bewildered expression off his face. That every cell in her body was crying out for a repeat of the spectacular performance of the other night was in direct conflict with what her mind told her that she should do in the interest of her own self-respect.

What she was feeling was the stuff of obsession.

What he apparently felt was of lust alone.

Neither was a suitable foundation for a loving and lasting relationship—something Lauren had been searching for in vain since her father's death. Rather than trying to go around Travis, she stood her ground with dignity as a myriad of emotions played across his face: desire, frustration and regret.

"I'm not looking to be your appetizer," Lauren finally said.

Travis felt like telling her to hang her own damned swing if that's the way she felt about it. But he couldn't.

Wouldn't.

He didn't want to put himself through the exquisite agony of watching her stretch out those long legs under that short pair of cutoffs and expose all her luscious curves to his ogling again. If previous bursts of her outrageous honesty hadn't already convinced him of Lauren's lack of guile, he might think she'd set out to deliberately torment him. But he wasn't even sure if she was aware of the effect she had on men in general.

But Travis knew.

Just this week he'd watched a string of deliverymen linger over a proffered glass of lemonade and fall all over themselves in an attempt to get her to notice them. He personally knew a dozen other men who gladly would line up on that porch for the opportunity to make themselves useful to such a beautiful woman looking for an exclusive relationship with any one of them. That Travis wasn't one of them was no reason for him to act as less than a gentleman. Throwing a temper tantrum just because she had made other plans wasn't likely to impress Lauren one little bit.

He took a step backward and removed his hands from her person.

"I didn't mean to offend you."

His tone was contrite. Under the circumstances, he supposed the fact that she didn't want anything further to do with him romantically was a credit to her character. He would have expected no less from his own sister had some commitment-shy man made her a similar offer.

"You didn't exactly offend me. It's just that—"

He cut Lauren off with the palm of his outstretched

hand. "Give me a minute to get my drill, and I'll make short order of this project."

Travis couldn't make out what she mumbled to his receding back, but by the time he returned with power tool in hand, she was tucked safely away in the cabin. As promised, it didn't take him any longer to hang her porch glider than it did for her to get ready for her presumed date. When she reappeared on the porch with a plate of food, Lauren was dressed to kill. She had on a little black dress that epitomized the word sexy. While not particularly daring in the cut of its hem or neckline, the crepe material clung suggestively to every curve of a body Travis had come to know intimately.

He despised the thought of other men drooling over her without him around to protect her.

"Don't you need a jacket?" he asked,

Lauren checked the sky for clouds. Finding none in sight, she shook her head. "I should be fine."

All signs of previous reasonableness on Travis's part disappeared.

"Not if you're thinking about going back to The Alibi," he told her in no uncertain terms.

"I'm not—at least not this evening."

With that, Lauren offered him a plate of food, but no further clues to her destination. Seeing the newly hung swing securely fastened, she gave Travis a smile that made him want to remodel the entire house.

"You have no idea how much I appreciate your help."

Travis felt himself melting like the cheese on the ham sandwich she handed him. It was piled high with thick slabs of meat and slathered with a delicious concoction of mayonnaise and horseradish. Fresh carrots and celery balanced out a mountain of homemade potato salad.

The woman certainly knew her way around a kitchen. And the bedroom, too.

"Don't you want to try it out?" he asked, gesturing to the masterpiece of suspended wood.

Gingerly Lauren took a seat and made room for him beside her.

"Only if you'll join me."

Travis obliged. He balanced his plate on his knees and took a healthy bite from his sandwich. When the swing didn't so much as creak at the strain of their combined weight, Lauren pushed off with the tip of one glittery high-heeled shoe. She seemed genuinely thrilled.

"Why, this is wonderful!"

Somehow the gentle rocking alleviated the tension between them in a way that words never could. Something about that soothing motion took Travis back to a simpler time: school days when he felt invincible and his grandfather had been waiting to share the details of his life. Days when a date was a date, a kiss was just a kiss and the only expectation a young man had was to have a good time without giving any thought to the future. Back then love was as uncomplicated as intercepting a touchdown pass.

The voice that interrupted his thoughts was as soft as the breeze that carried her subtle scent.

"I remember swinging on the porch with my dad when I was a little girl. We'd wait for the ice-cream truck to come by on hot summer afternoons and talk about all the fun things we were going to do together and what I wanted to be when I grew up. It didn't matter that my choice of occupations varied from week to week. Dad never belittled my dreams. I remember feeling so safe, so completely secure back then—before he died and my happy little world caved in around me."

"Tell me, Lauren, how do I make you feel?" Travis asked, taking her hand into his own.

As her friend, he told himself that he only wanted to share a sense of empathy over the loss of the only stable male in her life, a man he suspected attained superhero status from the very instant he first held his baby daughter in his arms. But there was nothing friendly about the frission of electrical energy zinging between them. That Travis actually wanted Lauren even more now than before they'd made love was proof of the intensity of his feelings for her.

Contrary to his expectations, sex had not made that persistent itch under his skin go away. In fact, it had only intensified it. No matter how hard he tried, Travis couldn't get this enigmatic woman out of his mind. And every time she popped into his thoughts, his body betrayed him. It seemed as if he'd been walking around in a permanent, embarrassing state of arousal ever since she'd spilled punch down his front and kissed him without any provocation whatsoever.

"I always feel safe when you're around," Lauren admitted with a sigh. "But when a girl turns into a woman, feeling secure becomes something more long-term in nature...."

The longing in her voice made Travis feel very small as she gazed across the open meadow to the snow-covered top of Haystack Mountain and opened her heart to him.

"What I'm looking for is a lifetime of holding hands with somebody on a swing like this one. And I get the distinct feeling that you don't want to be the person sitting here next to me growing old together."

A fist closed around Travis's throat. Not only could he imagine himself holding hands on this porch with Lauren, he also could envision a younger version of her snuggled up between.

"Daddy..." the little girl was sure to cajole, drawing the word into singsong syllables and melting him on the spot. *"Can I have...?"*

He'd always wanted to spoil a daughter, and the tender daydream stirred up old regrets and made him wistful. From ponies to sports cars, Travis doubted very much whether he'd be able to refuse his little girl much of anything when she looked up at him with sparkling green eyes the same color of her mother's. The same mesmerizing shade as Lauren's....

With the stealth of a silent stalker, fantasy collided with reality. He had no business thinking about having children with Lauren when the memory of what his ex-wife had done to their unborn baby drove a fist into his guts and left him gasping for air. Nothing could ever settle the debt his child had paid in their bloody war between the sexes. Nothing could atone for such a tragic loss in his life. He didn't deserve a second chance.

Travis let go of Lauren's hand. And of bygone dreams.

"You're right," he said, his voice suddenly sharp and bitter. "I'm definitely not the man you want sitting beside you on this swing for the rest of your life."

Nine

Lauren was hurt when Travis looked right through her as if she wasn't there. She couldn't imagine what she'd done to cause such a cold response from him. One minute they were sharing a cozy interlude and the next she was being vaporized by a look straight out of a horror movie. After Travis excused himself and took off with all the haste of a man fleeing the scene of a crime, Lauren checked her reflection in the mirror to see if she was still all there.

Would her own family even recognize the person staring back at her? That woman in the mirror looked far more self-assured and confident than Lauren felt at the moment. She almost decided to change into something more conservative for the evening when it oc-

curred to her that she was no longer content to fade into the background. Having swiveled men's heads for the
past couple of weeks, Lauren had come to appreciate the
attention. If Travis couldn't see past her old image that
was just too bad for him.

And if her family had any objections to the new and
improved Lauren, they would just have to get over them.

Her Aunt Hattie was throwing a Welcome Home party for the honeymooners down at Angelo's, the nicest
restaurant in town. Lauren figured it might as well suffice as her Coming Out party as well. Granted it, had
been quite some time since she'd turned sweet sixteen,
but she'd rather face all of the members of her extend-
ed family at once in her best dress as to endure their pro-
longed scrutiny one on one over the next several weeks.

Adjusting her bra strap and her attitude, she prepared
herself to face the gauntlet. She hoped her mother didn't
go ballistic over her short hair. And that Uncle Irve
didn't give her any grief over the length of her dress. And
that none of them had heard any whisperings about the
goings-on out at The Alibi or the Half Moon Ranch for
that matter. Her relatives liked to stand on propriety.

The Hewett family took up most of the seating available in Angelo's front room. When the waiter showed
Lauren to her party, she was met by both gasps of disbelief and exclamations of approval.

"What have you done to yourself?" people took turns
chiming as she took her seat.

Aunt Hattie didn't let her niece sit long. Lauren barely had time to place her order before her favorite aunt-

ie grabbed her by the elbow and asked to follow her to the ladies' room. Lauren's mother was a mere two steps behind. After sharing warm hugs and perfunctory information about how fabulous the honeymoon cruise had been, Barbara Aberdeen pressed her daughter for the details about her own life.

"You look stunning, honey!" she exclaimed.

Aunt Hattie butted in with her typical lack of patience for small talk. "To what—or rather to whom—do we owe this amazing transformation?"

Emboldened by their positive reaction, Lauren took a deep breath and gave them the unvarnished truth.

"To the fact that I've decided I want to get married."

Seeing their shocked expressions, she hastened to explain. "Not that I've actually met anyone so inclined to marry me—yet."

Her aunt and her mother shared a knowing look and a collective sigh.

"That's the attitude!" Hattie proclaimed.

"We've been waiting a long time for you to come to that decision, dear," Barbara Aberdeen added.

Before Lauren could give voice to her astonishment, her cute, perky, recently married cousin Marissa squeezed into the already crowded bathroom pretending the need to check her makeup.

"Tim's friend wants you to sit by him tonight," she told Lauren after adding her compliments about Lauren's makeover.

"His *single, eligible* friend, Jason," she added with a sly smile.

Lauren was flattered when Marissa asked who did her hair. It wasn't the first time she'd been asked that same question recently, and as always, she gave Claire a glowing endorsement. The young woman could open a shop in town with a ready-made clientele based on word of mouth alone. Lauren chatted with Marissa a few more minutes with a newfound sense of womanly camaraderie before rejoining the rest of the family.

Jason Wingate made room for Lauren beside him. "Tim never mentioned how lovely his wife's cousin was," he said.

Although his attentiveness was initially flattering, all too soon Lauren grew weary of his ingratiating patter. A short month ago, she would have been able to overlook Jason's weak chin and boring conversational skills. Having spent so much time with Travis lately, however, she had to fake interest in Jason's job as a loan officer at the local bank. Apparently rates were at an all time low, making home mortgages more affordable than ever. Unfortunately, Lauren had little interest either in Alan Greenspan or Jason Wingate.

She was in the midst of stifling a yawn when who should create a stir by simply walking into the room but Travis Banks himself! He discreetly slipped the waiter a bill to seat him at the table beside Lauren, then waved broadly to his old friend Henry Aberdeen.

Lauren's new stepfather greeted him with a big smile and a firm handshake.

"How was the honeymoon?" Travis asked.

"What are you doing here?" Lauren whispered under her breath as Henry launched into the highlights of the cruise.

"I didn't feel like cooking tonight," Travis responded. "Anything wrong with a man deciding to go out for dinner once in a while?"

Ever gracious, Barabara insisted that her husband's friend join them for dinner.

"Don't mind if I do," Travis said, gracing the room with an appreciative smile. He forced his chair between Jason's and Lauren's. "I don't much like eating alone."

"I mind," Lauren said between gritted teeth.

Ignoring her, Travis proceeded to charm her whole family—even Aunt Effie who usually took a cautious approach to everyone and everything. Having never seen him at his charismatic best except from a distance, Lauren cast distrustful looks his way. He laughed at her nephew John's stupid knock-knock jokes, complimented her mother on her bridal glow, joshed with her cousins and offered to pay the bill for the entire party in return for the simple pleasure of their company. It was all Lauren could do to refrain from pushing aside the arm he draped so affably over her shoulder.

Or aiming a dinner roll at his head.

For the life of her, she couldn't figure out what he was doing here—other than ruining her chances with a man she wasn't at all interested in.

Travis himself wasn't quite sure why he had crashed this party. He knew only that the heart wants what it wants and that right now, it wanted to make sure Lau-

ren wasn't meeting some other man who might just be
willing to offer her what he couldn't—a long-term commitment. Lauren hadn't left the ranch fifteen minutes
before he'd started getting all twisted up inside just
thinking of her on a date. Something about that little
black dress she wore left a lasting impression, and the
thought of her wearing it for someone else made him
go just a little bit crazy.

Crazy enough to follow her into town on the pretense
of needing groceries. Crazy enough to give the bartender down at The Alibi twenty bucks to call him if she
showed up there later. Crazy enough to drive all over
Pinedale searching the streets for any sign of her car.
Crazy enough to march right inside Angelo's to see just
exactly who she was out cavorting with and to do everything in his power to ruin her date.

That it turned out Lauren was spending time with her
family didn't lessen the threat that Jason Wingate
poised. In fact it only intensified Travis's concern. That
he actually liked her family didn't make it any easier for
him to dismiss a growing sense of guilt. That he felt so
at ease among such a diverse group of well-meaning
people so obviously devoted to Lauren's happiness
didn't alter the probability that none of them would
likely approve of her being used by a man who only
wanted her body at his convenience.

Travis was not too ashamed of himself to keep from
plying her with liquor though. He ordered her a stiff
drink hoping the alcohol might soften up those hard,
searching looks she kept giving him. When she knocked

the first one back like it was little more than water, he promptly ordered her another.

"Anytime you'd like to take a trail ride around Fremont Lake just let me know," Travis offered everyone in the room. "I've got plenty of horses and the fishing's great there this time of year. Maybe you all could even convince Lauren to come along."

"Fat chance," she mumbled under her breath.

"He's adorable," Aunt Hattie mouthed to her niece.

"And so handsome," her mother added behind her hand.

Lauren rolled her eyes.

Travis grinned. He was having a great time. Lauren's family was loud and funny and protective. As different from his stuffy ex-in-laws as Lauren was from Jaclyn herself. No wonder Lauren had such a good sense of humor and so much faith in her ability to accomplish whatever she put her mind to.

Henry winked and leaned over to whisper in his ear. "If she's anything like her mother, you'll have your hands full."

Travis had never seen his old friend look happier.

"Now, Henry, don't read more into my friendship with Lauren than is there."

Henry wasn't dissuaded from issuing a warning of his own. "Just be sure you treat her right," he added, all traces of humor gone from his eyes. "I'm as fond of Lauren as if I were her actual father."

It had been a long time since Travis had considered anyone who he was pursuing as someone's daughter.

The thought brought him up short. He didn't want to alienate Henry or look bad in Lauren's relatives' eyes.

Or hurt her, either.

Nonetheless, he found her sudden aloofness disconcerting. Unlike the gold digger he'd divorced, Lauren clearly wasn't looking to marry for either money or status. She appeared content with her modest teaching salary and seemed to take inordinate delight in her newfound sense of independence. To a man who'd grown distrustful of the entire female gender, Lauren's straightforward motives for wanting to get married seemed much too transparent.

Jason strained to see around Travis who had somehow managed to be in his way all evening. Looking utterly exasperated, he finally gave up.

"Well, I guess I should be going," he announced. "Would you like me to drive you home, Lauren?"

"Thank you for offering, but I've got my own car," she said sounding genuinely sorry.

The note of regret in Lauren's voice bothered Travis. Stirred by a fierce and rare sense of jealousy, he was glad he wasn't going to have to challenge Jason for the privilege of driving her home—although the thought of driving his fist through the other man's face gave him an inordinate sense of pleasure. Not a man who was usually given to violent outbursts, he wondered what exactly was happening to him.

"I'll call you soon," Jason promised Lauren. He shot Travis a killing glance over his shoulder as he took his leave.

While Lauren was preoccupied with saying her goodbyes, Travis discretely slipped her keys into his own pocket. Her relatives nodded approvingly when later in the evening he insisted on driving her home himself. He put a hand up to ward off her resistance and chastened her in a tone that caused steam to come out of her ears.

"I'm sorry, darlin', but you've had too much to drink, and being close neighbors as we are, it's not at all out of my way to drop you at your place. I'd be more than happy to drive you back into town in the morning to retrieve your car if that puts your mind at ease any."

"That is so thoughtful of you, dear," Barbara Aberdeen clucked, looking like she was tempted to pinch his cheeks.

Lauren made a mad grab for the set of keys Travis dangled in front of her face and uttered an unladylike oath under her breath when he snatched them away.

"You are insufferable," she told him through lips pressed tightly into a smile for the sake of maintaining family harmony in the too public setting.

Quite certain her mother would be horrified to discover just how neighborly they actually had been, Lauren demurely accepted Travis's hand at the small of her back as he directed her to the front door. To curious bystanders they looked like the perfect couple: he so rugged and handsome and she so pretty with that bright flush of color upon her cheeks.

The instant they were outside Lauren wheeled upon Travis with the ferocity of a pit bull.

"What exactly do you think you're doing?" she demanded. Premeditated murder glittered in her eyes.

"Just making sure you get home safe and sound," Travis drawled, full of honey and phony concern.

"Don't you mean safe, sound and *alone?*" she asked, sarcastically mimicking his twang as they reached the curb where he'd parked his vehicle.

Had Lauren not been so furious, she might have found his unexpected display of jealousy amusing. Had she been a more devious type, she might have used that to her advantage. As it was, she simply couldn't fathom someone as good looking and accomplished as Travis Banks being threatened the least little bit by a man like Jason. All evening long she'd found herself comparing the two men, with Jason soundly losing on every count save one: his sincerity.

She chastised herself for being so judgmental. After all, Jason was a definite improvement over Fenton Marsh. He was a nice person. He had a good job and he didn't bring a truckload of emotional baggage into a relationship. During the course of their conversation earlier, Jason even indicated that he was looking to settle down—if the right woman came along.

"No," Travis clarified. "I don't necessarily think you should go home *alone.*"

The suggestive tone of those words made Lauren go all mushy inside as he tipped his head and made his intentions known. Tingles of anticipation shot through her. His lips brushed against hers, and she felt a familiar warmth invade her body. All of a sudden Lauren forgot all about being mad. Wrapping her arms around his neck, she matched him thrust for thrust in a ritualistic dance as ageless as all the lovers who had gone before them.

"Definitely not alone," Travis reiterated, reluctantly taking his moist lips from hers at the sound of a carload of teenagers honking their horn and hooting as they raced by.

That couldn't possibly be their homeroom teacher making a spectacle of herself on Main Street of all places. Could it?

Lauren's face grew hot as Travis helped her up into her seat by strategically placing his hand squarely on her bottom and giving her a little boost. After he was settled behind the wheel, she gestured to the rowdy youngsters peeling out at the next stoplight.

"More grist for the rumor mill."

"I have an idea," Travis said, flashing her a smile. "Let's give them something really juicy to talk about."

Clearly he was not as mortified as Lauren by the thought of people gossiping about them. She attempted to explain the gravity of the situation to him without sounding prudish.

"That's all well and fine for you to say. *You* don't have to face those young men in your classroom next fall. Or their parents. Or the principal who told Lucia Mote that it would be in her best interest to marry the man she was 'shacking up' with."

Travis looked shocked. The Spanish teacher's elopement was news to him. As was the part that the principal played in making it happen.

"This is the new millennium," he reminded Lauren. "Not the turn of the nineteenth century."

"Yes, but this is a conservative community and an administrator can get rid of anyone he wants to if he has enough pressure to do so."

Lauren knew. She had recently been assigned to a Drama Review Board because certain influential people had objected to the director's last production on the grounds that some lines were too racy for a public school performance. Lauren herself felt forced to walk a fine line regarding the selection of literature that she used in her own classes. Teaching *The Scarlet Letter* could become uncomfortable if people decided to compare her to the novel's beleaguered heroine.

"You're blowing this all out of proportion," Travis insisted.

But for the remainder of the ride home he made no move toward her that could be misconstrued by anyone—including Lauren herself. Unfortunately, having gotten exactly what she'd asked for, she started having second thoughts. Travis's sudden restraint was no deterrent to her own reaction to his nearness. The effect of the kiss with which he'd branded her showed no signs of diminishing. Her lips tingled, and her blood ran hot. She was on fire.

Arriving home before she had a chance to gather her wits about her, Lauren felt an awkwardness that had hitherto been absent in their relationship. And she was filled with a jarring sense of grief at the thought of spending the night alone.

She wondered what harm could come of indulging her body's demands one more time. It wasn't as though she was a virgin who was saving herself for her wedding night. Or even as though it would be their first time together. She'd heard that nothing was better, more bittersweet and satisfying than break-up sex.

"Damn you!" she exclaimed, unsnapping her seat belt with an impatient flick of her wrist.

Travis couldn't have looked any more startled when she leaned across the seat and assertively pressed a kiss on him. Not pausing to question the mercurial nature of her mood swings, he dragged her out of the pick up and swept her up in his arms. The next thing Lauren knew, she was being carried over the threshold of her cabin, vaguely aware that this romantic gesture was part of the matrimonial tradition that she unfortunately would never have with the man who held her so lightly in his arms. However, that knowledge was not enough to give Lauren the strength to stop the inevitable from happening.

Bodies tangled with sheets as Travis laid her upon the bed. The last time they'd made love, he had taken special care to be tender. Today neither one of them showed any inclination toward anything but hot and wild sex with no emotional strings attached. Lauren tugged her dress over her head and kicked her high heels to the far corner of the room. Travis tore off his shirt and pants, struggling to remove his boots first. Lauren's sexy matching bra and panties were lost upon him as she ripped them off without regard to the indecent price she'd paid for them.

Neither was concerned with preening at the moment. Or protection. Nothing, except complete, immediate gratification, counted for much. All worries and inhibitions, all ties to rational consequences dissolved beneath the flesh's consuming needs. Naked, they sought refuge in the glorious sensation of skin against skin. Animal sounds accompanied pure animal lust as selfish pleasure gave way to selfish pleasure.

Lauren grabbed her brass headboard between both hands and commanded in a hoarse whisper, "Now!"

Travis obliged. Already fully aroused, there was no reason for foreplay on his account. She unabashedly held herself open, and he slipped inside with an eagerness he thought he'd outgrown. Slick with sweat, they moved in unison, each working toward a shared goal. That Lauren could climax so quickly and so often in such a short time was a wonderment to her.

And an incredible turn-on to him.

"Oh, baby," was all he could manage before exploding in time to yet another of her over-the-top orgasms.

Lauren opened her eyes wide to watch him. He was so very beautiful in the throes of passion. To hold such a gorgeous man between her legs and claim him as a willing and alluring partner in her own right was the stuff of fantasies. His breath came in great whooshes that stirred the bangs out of her face and made her feel incredibly powerful. He shuddered in exquisite release. The warmth that flooded Lauren satisfied her as a woman—and made her want to have his babies.

A whole passel of them.

The realization that might actually be a possibility considering their lack of foresight in the birth control department didn't slack on her desire one whit. Figuring the damage had already been done in regard to potential conception, Lauren tossed aside such worries with a carelessness that was uncharacteristic of her. She didn't think this was the right time of the month for her to conceive and didn't particularly give a damn if it was. She just wanted the wonderful feeling of being in Travis's arms to stay with her forever. Wrapping her legs around his middle, she gave a squeeze to let him know she wasn't ready to let him go just yet.

"Again?" she asked, hoping to prolong the moment when he left her bed and went home unencumbered by thoughts of her.

Travis's chuckle gave the impression he was amused by the insatiable monster he had created. "You might have to give me a minute,"

Licking the salt of his sweat from his neck, Lauren teased him into a state of arousal far sooner than one would have imagined possible after such incredible earth shattering sex. She was a wildcat, suggesting positions and offering to do things that most men only dreamed of. By the time she was done turning Travis into liquid honey, he couldn't have straggled out of bed had he wanted to.

Completely and utterly satisfied, they snuggled in each other's arms, not wanting to lose the feeling of closeness and togetherness that they both knew could be so very short-lived. Lauren was as surprised as Travis that desire could well up inside her so quickly after each successive climax. She cherished the tender petting of after-play as much as, if not more than, the act of intercourse itself. She had read somewhere that some women could ride out multiple orgasms, each gaining in momentum and intensity. She would never have guessed she was one of those lucky few. Lauren hoped that didn't make her a nymphomaniac.

Figuring that she had nothing to lose, other than her pride, she decided to take advantage of her lover's spent state to risk her heart.

"I could take a lifetime of loving like this."

Travis tensed in her arms, and Lauren immediately regretted uttering the words that ruined an otherwise perfect moment. He removed the arm he'd possessively thrown over her and rolled away. Draping one sexy, well-defined, slightly hairy leg over the edge of the bed, he sat up and cradled his head in his hands, giving the impression that he was fighting off a headache—namely her. Lauren sat up as well and reached out to give his shoulder a reassuring pat.

"I'm sorry."

And yet, having broached this sensitive subject, she couldn't let it just go at that. Sighing, she drew her knees and the top sheet up under her chin before posing a delicate question.

"Just what is it that you are so afraid of, Travis?"

Ten

Travis didn't like being put on the spot, especially when he couldn't come up with a reasonable answer to the very question he'd been asking himself for the past few days. In any case, he didn't think it wise to continue this particular discussion in the nude. Lauren's lovely body made it impossible for him to concentrate. To make matters worse, he swore he could almost hear her ovaries ringing the wedding march. Cursing himself for failing to use protection in the fervor of the moment, he just hoped she wasn't pregnant.

Or did he?

The thought of fathering a baby with this woman was not altogether unappealing. In fact, the warm glow he felt deep inside gave him reason to pause. But, having been pushed into a bad marriage before by a woman who used her pregnancy as a lifetime meal ticket and then discarded his baby as if it were no more than a cancelled stub, Travis was leery of making the same mistake again. After his divorce, he'd promised himself never to let his libido overcome logical, rational thought again.

That promise might as well have been written in the sand for all the good it had done him tonight.

You would think that a man would have better sense to try filling his canteen from a poisoned creek after nearly dying there before. Travis knew his reluctance to commit was inexplicably tied to his disastrous relationship with Jaclyn, but he suspected the root causes went even deeper. The best he could manage by way of answering Lauren's question about what he was so afraid of was to simply quote the Rolling Stones.

"Once bitten, twice shy."

Torn between wanting to remain in bed with Lauren forever and running as fast as he could in the opposite direction, he took her face between the palms of his work-roughened hands. With her hair tousled and her lips swollen from his kisses, she was the most beautiful creature he'd ever seen. Her very soul seemed to shimmer in the depth of those guileless eyes. Try as Travis might to rationalize away what they shared as nothing more than great sex, the knowledge that it was much, much more resonated deep in the marrow of his bones.

And scared the hell out of him.

He didn't feel inclined to admit that to the woman staring at him with those big soft eyes and an expression of concern splashed all over her pretty face. Travis wasn't much for confiding his fears with anyone, let alone the person he most wanted to impress with his stoic machismo. When Lauren ventured a response to that old refrain, he chastised with a single finger placed upon her lips.

"Shhh… Let's not ruin what we have by overanalyzing things."

Instantly the expression on her face turned inscrutable.

"Fine."

The defeat in that single syllable made Travis feel guiltier than any amount or quality of argumentation that she might have offered to convince him his fears were groundless.

"It isn't like I promised you more than—" he began to say defensively.

"I said fine."

Travis exhaled loudly. "What's so wrong with staying in a holding pattern for a little while?" he asked. "Don't you think it would be smart to get to know each other a little better before we jump into something rash?"

Lauren freed herself of his hold and whipped the sheet back.

"You seem to think you know me plenty well enough, but whenever I try to understand you better, you pull away so fast and hard that it makes my head spin. If you ask me, I think you're stuck in a permanent holding pattern and are just too afraid to land."

Distracted by Lauren's state of undress, Travis placed

a kiss on the top of her nose and did his best to defuse the situation.

"Come on," he cajoled. "You really don't want to weasel a commitment out of me that I'm not ready to give just yet. And…"

The cuckoo clock on the wall popped out of his hole to remind them that time was tick, tick, ticking onward.

"And," he continued, clearing his throat and staring into hurt eyes. "I don't want to lose you, either. Maybe we could try finding a compromise that we both can live with."

Curiosity softened the stubborn set of Lauren's jaw. She tilted her head to one side and gave him her full attention.

"I'm listening."

Travis had a hard time forming his thoughts into a coherent sentence. What he was about to suggest was in itself more of a commitment than he was sure he was ready for.

"What do you think about moving into the big house with me?"

Lauren blinked. She studied him closely for some time before responding. She, too, was having a hard time getting words around the heart stuck in her throat. Except for the fact that Travis stopped short of actually asking her to marry him, the idea of moving in with him was a dream come true. Her pulse zinged. The blood pounded in her ears. And somewhere in the distance an angel choir burst into a chorus of hallelujahs.

And yet she hesitated.

She didn't know what was wrong with her. Any woman in her right mind would jump up and down at such an opportunity to cohabitate with this gorgeous hunk of man. Lauren had to ask herself why she would throw up a blockade against happiness rather than rushing to embrace it with open arms. The easy answer to that question was simply to blame everyone else for the expectations that she put upon herself.

"I've already told you that my position as a public school teacher makes that difficult," she said.

There was, of course, more to it than that, but she didn't want to divulge anything more personal. How could she ever hope to explain that the person she was most afraid of disappointing was actually her father? Gone for many years now, his presence still guided all his daughter's major decisions. And left her reaching for a higher standard than others.

Travis dismissed her concern with a blunt question. "Who's to know whether you're in this little house as my renter or living in the big house as my lover?"

As logical as that sounded, something queasy sloshing around in the pit of Lauren's stomach made her nervous about agreeing too quickly.

"I'd know," she told him unequivocally. "And my family would be certain to find out sooner or later. It's not like we live in a sprawling cosmopolitan center instead of a small community where everybody knows everybody else's business. Somehow, I doubt my relatives would be very open-minded about the kind of living arrangements that don't involve a ring."

The thought that her father would roll over in his grave at the news of his little girl shacking up with the most notorious player in all the county didn't make her feel any better about wanting to accept his offer. For one silly moment before Travis had opened his mouth, she'd thought he was actually on the verge of proposing. Swallowing her disappointment, Lauren wondered why his compromise couldn't at least include setting a wedding date—even one way off in the future. That alone would be enough to appease her family, squelch any rumors floating around town, buy Travis himself some time to warm up to the idea of marriage—and assuage her own stubborn feminine pride.

It was that very sense of pride that prevented Lauren from asking Travis for any token of his fidelity. Having just initiated the wild sexual interlude that preceded this conversation, it wasn't that she was afraid of asserting herself. She had certainly proven herself an apt aggressor in bed. But Travis was right about the folly of forcing a man into a commitment he didn't want.

In the innermost chambers of her romantic core, Lauren longed for a Hollywood proposal upon bended knee. And not one coerced by threats or tears or wheedling, either. She wanted Travis to ask her to marry him because he wanted to. Because, like her, he couldn't imagine living without her.

He cleared his throat. "You know it hasn't been easy for me getting over my divorce. Jaclyn was the kind of woman who always had to be in control of everything—regardless of how I felt about matters large or small…."

Lauren couldn't know that he was envisioning the baby he'd never hold. Travis never talked about this part of his life with anyone. Not even his lawyer who demanded to know all the pertinent information that would advance his case in court. His voice sounded as rough as sandpaper as he continued.

"When I finally filed for divorce, Jaclyn made things as messy as she could. She had a… miscarriage… and we never seemed able to recover from the loss."

Travis didn't mention that the miscarriage hadn't been spontaneous and he was not part of the decision of whether they were going to keep the baby or not. He saw no point in disparaging his ex-wife or bringing up hurtful topics that no amount of discussion would ever change—other than to give Lauren some idea of why he was so hesitant to embrace the concept of marriage.

"Suffice it to say that until you literally waltzed into my life, I haven't wanted to get close to anyone. So just in case you're not aware of it, asking you to move in is a big step for me."

Lauren didn't know what to say. Travis's life was so much more complicated than she had ever imagined. It had been so hard for her to deal with the loss of her father. She couldn't fathom what it would be like to lose a child. Her heart went out to him. And to herself.

If she was having this much trouble broaching the subject of marriage, how was she supposed to casually bring up the fact that she wanted children someday, too? Lauren knew that Travis would make a wonderful father. She wondered how he felt about starting over. With her.

She supposed she should feel grateful that a man so publicly sworn to bachelorhood would offer to share his home with her, but somehow she wasn't feeling particularly lucky. As important as it was that they continue this discussion about his first marriage in greater depth, Lauren could tell by his stony expression that Travis had said all he was going to say on the matter for the time being. Reaching deep inside herself, she offered him a little smile and postponed the conversation that was already twisting her guts into tight, hard knots.

She patted the pillow beside her. "Why don't you come on back to bed and we'll both sleep on it? Hopefully a good night's sleep will do wonders for both of our perspectives."

Apparently happy enough to leave things at that, Travis snuggled back under the covers and dozed off almost immediately. Lauren remained wide-awake, however. She didn't want to dismiss his offer out of hand.

Still, she couldn't help feeling diminished by the compromise he suggested. It wasn't so much her fear of God or even of what the neighbors might say as much as it was a sense that she was worth more than he was willing to give her. Afraid of selling herself short in the long run, Lauren believed that she deserved a soul mate who would openly claim her.

She couldn't help but wonder if Travis didn't want to keep their relationship hidden away from his friends and family because he was secretly ashamed of her. Maybe he couldn't get past her nerdy image from the past. Perhaps it was merely the sexist belief that he didn't have to buy the cow if the milk was free. Or did he simply think she was too old for happily ever afters complete with white dresses and fairy godmothers?

Or was he merely looking for an invisible playmate and no one fit that description more perfectly than she?

Lauren felt herself fading away at the thought.

And fought against it.

She had worked too hard to make herself visible to the world to let such negative thoughts destroy her new self-image. Yet as tempting as it was to walk away from this relationship while she could still hold her head up, the thought of abandoning what she had with Travis was almost more than she could bear. Hoping that she would be better able to face that possibility in the morning light, she tried to put her fears to rest. In the bleak and lonely hours of the night, it was enough to cuddle up in this man's loving arms and feel his heart beating against her own without asking for more.

Unfortunately, sleep did little to shed any light on her dilemma. When Lauren woke early the next morning, she was no closer to knowing what to do than she'd been the night before. If anything, she was even more confused. Unlike her, Travis hadn't lost any sleep over the issue. Reveling in the sensation of waking up after a good night's sleep, he stretched his long, masculine body out so that his feet stuck out over the foot of her queen-size bed. And wriggled his hairy toes.

"Good morning, beautiful," he said, rolling over on his side to look at her directly.

All sinew and muscle and latent strength, he was too good-looking for words.

"Morning, sleepyhead," she managed to reply.

Quite frankly Lauren was a little irritated that he'd slept so well. That he seemed so sure of himself. That he seemed so apparently unattached to whatever decision she reached in regard to their future. That he didn't seem to doubt for a moment that she had already mentally packed her bags and would be moving in with him just as soon as she could gather up her things.

As tempting as that thought was, Lauren really hadn't made up her mind yet. In fact, the only thing she knew for sure was that she didn't want to slip back into a state of invisibility just to make life easier for others.

"Well, angel, have you come to any conclusions?" he asked, stroking her bare arm lovingly.

Lauren pushed a wayward lock of dark hair away from the face she loved. She knew she would be doing a terrible disservice to Travis, not to mention herself, by not honestly disclosing her feelings for him. Squeaky with apprehension, her voice betrayed the depth of those feeling as she reached inside herself for an ounce of courage.

"Just one."

Travis trailed a lazy finger along the edge of the sheet where it bulged out to accommodate the swell of her breasts.

"And what's that?" he asked.

Swallowing hard, Lauren looked straight into a pair of eyes that had captivated her for so much of her life. She wanted nothing less than his full attention when she spoke the words aloud for the first time. She held his gaze tenderly.

"That I love you."

A chasm of silence accompanied that heartfelt proclamation.

It wasn't exactly the reaction Lauren had been hoping for. She thought the least Travis could do was to say something. Anything. It seemed his mouth was temporarily under construction. Blinking back her tears, she willed him to look away so she could make a graceful getaway. She'd never felt so stupid or ugly or embarrassed in all her life.

"You don't have to say anything back," she somehow managed to croak out before climbing out of bed, taking the sheet along with her. "I just thought you should know that I wouldn't move in with you if I didn't love you. That's all."

That's all?

Reeling from Lauren's announcement, Travis didn't know why he couldn't bring himself to say the words that she was longing to hear. It would be so easy to staunch her tears with a lie, but he didn't want to hurt her any more than he already had by giving her false hope.

Only the crazy thing was Travis wasn't so sure he would be lying to repeat those three little words. He knew that what he felt for this woman went far beyond lust; otherwise he never would have asked her to move in with him. It went far beyond simple attraction and genuine fondness, too. And it went far beyond what his battered heart could accept.

Was it too much to believe a woman as special as Lauren could truly love him for who he was, not just what he represented? Not for all the things he could buy her or for the social perks associated with a name synonymous with one of the biggest ranches in Wyoming.

If anything, the truth was far more frightening than any lie he might feel compelled to tell at the moment.

Travis reached out to grab a fistful of quickly disappearing sheet. He pulled Lauren back into bed where he held her a little too tightly—as though he were afraid that she would fly away if he gave her half a chance. He understood that her unexpected proclamation of love didn't necessarily mean she was willing to move in with him, either. As much as that thought annoyed him, he secretly had to admire her character. Few women he knew would consider the offer a moral dilemma.

"I don't deserve you," he said, glad to discover his mouth was up and running again.

Still, his voice sounded as gravelly as the road connecting them to the rest of the world.

"You probably don't," Lauren agreed, hiding her tears behind the border of the sheet wrapped toga style around her.

"Does that mean you're not going to move in with me?"

Lauren studied the quality of light filtering through

the window. She followed a dust mite that crossed the path of her eye. Tested the springy texture of the fine hair along Travis's arm against her fingers.

"It means that I want to, but I'd like to think about it a little while longer before I let you know for sure."

Hurt that she wasn't happier about the prospect of living with him, Travis grew uneasy at the idea of Lauren weighing the pros and cons of such a decision with anyone else. Just thinking about her broaching this touchy subject with her mother or stepfather Henry, who'd already warned him about hurting her, or any of the other funny, sweet relatives who loved her so openly made him feel like a real heel.

A heel that had stepped in cow manure and didn't have the good sense to scrape it off before he got to smelling too bad.

He supposed that's what he got for falling for someone with scruples

"Big girls don't have to check in with their mommies before they make up their own minds," he pointed out.

That Travis really liked Lauren's family complicated things. He didn't want to come between Lauren and the people whose opinions meant the most to her. He didn't particularly want them thinking badly of him, either. Or make her already difficult teaching job any more challenging for that matter.

Suddenly a horrible thought occurred to him.

"You're not going to talk to your principal about this, are you?" he wanted to know.

If that fat, bald, mealy-mouthed old goat had anything to say about this, he could damn well say it to Travis—right before he ate his fist.

Lauren shook her head. "Not unless he brings it up."

Travis was okay with that. School wouldn't start up for another couple of months, and by then who knew how their relationship would be progressing? Experience had taught him that it was one thing to date someone and quite another to live with her. It hadn't taken long to realize the honeymoon was over with Jaclyn shortly after it had begun. He truly believed that the wisest course for any couple considering marriage was to try living together first on a temporary basis.

Not that Travis was predicting failure for the trial arrangement he was suggesting. A veteran of the war between the sexes, he was simply preparing himself for it, just in case.

Eleven

"What a quandary!" Suzanne exclaimed in mock exaggeration. Holding out both hands, she mimed a scale and proceeded to weigh her friend's options. "Let's see, should I move in with some gorgeous, rich hunk who curls my toes with his kisses, or should I live out the rest of my days alone and miserable as the spinster of Pinedale High?"

The image evoked in Lauren's mind a disturbing cross between the Old Maid and the lead character from *Phantom of the Opera*.

Continuing on, Suzanne dropped her left hand to her side as if it couldn't possibly support the weight of the obvious answer. "Gosh, I don't know. What should I do?"

Lauren worried her bottom lip between her teeth. "Do you really think it's that simple?" she asked.

"Yes, I do."

Lauren wished she had Suzanne's decisive outlook on life. If only matters of the heart could be as easily resolved as her friend made it sound. Of course, giving advice was far different from living it.

"I didn't see you moving in with Mike before the two of you got married," Lauren pointed out.

A coy smile curled Suzanne's lips. "True," she admitted. "But then Mike wasn't as afraid of commitment as Travis. In fact, as I recall he couldn't hustle me up the aisle fast enough to suit his timetable."

A faraway look came across Suzanne's face and she sighed with a wistfulness one rarely heard in her voice.

"Those were the days. Back when paying bills didn't take precedence over making love."

Although Lauren commiserated, she really couldn't empathize. From the outside looking in, her friend had the perfect marriage. It was hard not to envy the spur-of-the-moment elopement that had shocked the whole town and marked the beginning of Suzanne and Mike's life together.

"At least you don't have to be afraid of Mike leaving you whenever he feels like it. When you live with somebody, who's to say the least little argument won't lead to terminating the entire relationship?"

Suzanne pushed a cup of coffee toward Lauren and offered her free refills on the advice she was about to give.

"Look, Lauren, I know you're afraid of operating without a net. That you're worried if you move in, Travis will think that he's pacified you and things will deteriorate the instant you say you're ready for more of a commitment. You need to realize that marriage is no guarantee that won't happen, either. People do get divorced. Travis did. And that's probably why he wants to start out slow and easy. Remember love is a choice. It's hard work. And above all, love is worth the risk."

Lauren appreciated the insight and support. Having waited a long time herself for the right man to come along, Suzanne wasn't one to give flippant counsel. It meant a lot to know that whatever the consequences of her decision Lauren always would have a friend to lean on. She sighed in anticipation of what lay ahead of her.

"I just hope Mom is as open-minded when I broach this subject."

She fretted for the better part of the morning before dragging her feet to the doorstep of her mother's house. Lauren stopped by the bakery first and purchased a dozen glazed donuts just in case she needed something to soften Barbara Aberdeen up. Out of sheer nervousness, Lauren ate three of them herself on the way over.

"Good Lord," her mother exclaimed, opening the door. "You don't have to ring the doorbell like some stranger."

Lauren didn't know how to explain that she'd been afraid of interrupting something intimate. After dancing around the real reason for the visit, she finally brought up the subject in an awkward, roundabout way and steeled herself for the explosion to come.

"Why, that's wonderful news, honey!" Barbara exclaimed throwing her arms around her daughter.

It turned out that Lauren's mother was far less conservative than she had thought. In fact, as the conversation wore on, Lauren couldn't help being just a little hurt that her mother seemed more concerned about Travis's feelings than hers.

"You can't blame a man who went through the kind of nasty divorce that Travis did for being a little gun shy. I'd advise against giving him any kind of ultimatum. You know that any man worth his salt will resist that kind of emotional blackmail."

"You mean you wouldn't be disappointed in me if I skipped the wedding and went straight to the honeymoon?" Lauren asked, sounding far more incredulous and naive than she wanted to.

"You could never disappoint me, dear. I thought you knew that."

Her response was so instantaneous and sincere that it made Lauren teary. She dabbed at her eyes with her fingertips.

"I'm sorry. I seem to be doing a lot of crying lately. It's just not like me."

Barbara gave her another hug before leaving to fetch a box of tissues. She sat down beside her daughter on the couch, pulled a couple of tissues from the floral print box, and pressed them into her Lauren's hand.

"What I want to know is whether you love him."

"God help me, I do, Mom. I love him so much it hurts."

Barbara looked perplexed. "Then I don't see what the problem is."

What had been merely a trickle of tears turned into a river as Lauren struggled to admit the awful truth. Just the memory of that pregnant pause when she'd told Travis she loved him sent mascara cascading down her face. Her words caught on swallowed sobs. She couldn't imagine her father ever treating her mother so horribly and didn't know how to put her humiliation into words.

"I'm afraid he doesn't love me back."

"There, there," her mother said, trying to comfort her baby the best she knew how. "A man doesn't ask you to move in with him unless he feels something for you. Maybe Travis just isn't very demonstrative about his feelings. Some men aren't you know. Some men simply defy pigeonholing. Henry says such nice things about Travis, and he seemed to fit into the family so well the other night. Leta and the boys are all fired up to take him up on his generous offer to go horseback riding."

"Who cares how he fits into the rest of the family?" Lauren wailed. "I'm more concerned about whether he wants to fit in with me. I want him to want what I want. And what I want is for him to want to marry me."

Lauren's head was beginning to spin. She wasn't sure her words were making any sense.

"The problem is," she continued on, "that I just don't think there's any way that I can make that happen."

Barbara reached out in empathy. It clearly hurt her very much to see her only child in such pain. "I wish there was something I could do to make this easier for you, but I can't. I can only encourage you to think about giving Travis a chance to make you happy. To let love flower in its own time. To advise you not to try to force things. And to let you know that I'll support you no matter what you decide to do with the rest of your life."

Having never in a million years expected her mother to sanction any kind of sexual activity outside the bounds of marriage, Lauren was speechless. Between Suzanne and her mom, all the obstacles in the way of Lauren accepting Travis's offer were falling away faster than she could erect new ones. There was only one person left whose opinion mattered more to her than anyone else's.

And he wasn't around to offer any advice.

"What do you suppose Daddy would think?" she asked, sniffling into a tissue.

A tender smile crossed Barbara's face. "He'd want you to be happy. I know for a fact that he wouldn't want you to sacrifice your own joy out of some misguided sense of obligation to his memory. Over the years I'm afraid in your mind you've elevated your father to sainthood, but never forget that he was made of flesh and blood just like you and me. I think he would have liked Travis very much. I do."

Lauren brightened. Her mother was a pretty good judge of character. "You do?"

"In a lot of ways, he reminds me of your father who, by the way, was more than a little nervous about walking down the aisle himself. The truth is, I wasn't absolutely sure he was going to show up at the church on the day of our wedding."

Lauren couldn't believe what she was hearing. The

way she remembered her father telling it, he'd fallen in love with pretty Barbara Miller at first sight and immediately begun doing everything humanly possible to tie the knot binding her to him as quickly as possible.

"And," her mother continued in a gentle tone that belied the seriousness of what she was about to say. "I know that you have some intimacy issues. Listen to me, Lauren. Just because your father died doesn't mean that Travis is going to leave you, too. If your father's death teaches you anything, it should be to celebrate life for all it's worth while you can."

Having a spotlight cast into the deepest, darkest closet of her mind was illuminating—not to mention a little embarrassing. Suddenly, all Lauren's fears seemed stupid and small as it became perfectly clear that the decision to take a chance on love was entirely her own.

The fact that everybody she confided in seemed crazy about Travis should have made her decision to put her misgivings aside all that much easier.

But for some reason it didn't.

And that in itself was testimony to the depth of her girlish attachment to fairy-tale endings and an aversion to reality when it came complete with warts. Clearly no one else had a problem with Travis's proposal but Lauren herself.

She had some serious soul searching to do. The chances of that occurring if she returned home and found Travis in her bed were highly unlikely. Thinking wasn't something she did well around him, particularly when he was naked. So when she left her mother's house and turned her car, not in the direction of the Half Moon Ranch but rather in the exact opposite direction, Lauren wasn't worried about getting lost. She had enough money in her pocket to cover her expenses while she sorted out the doubts in her heart and tried to get her head screwed on straight. Any decent motel should be able to offer her what she needed most: solitude and room service.

Driving helped soothe her frayed nerves. The open road embraced her. Lauren's sense of foreboding rolled back with every click of the odometer. The open range offered breathing space and miles and miles of uninterrupted contemplation beneath a cloudless Wyoming sky that put no ceiling on a person's dreams. She made a game of following any road that appealed to her sense of adventure.

Tiredness from lack of sleep the previous night combined with the emotional exhaustion of sorting through her feelings. Completely used up both physically and emotionally, Lauren shut off her cell phone without a sense of guilt. She certainly wasn't married, and had yet to commit to moving in with Travis on a temporary basis. A grown woman she didn't need anyone's permission to take a little road trip.

When Lauren finally pulled into a quaint bed-and-breakfast tucked into the foothills of the Tetons, she gave herself permission to sleep for days on end. She had just collected her room key when a handsome stranger registering next to her in the hotel lobby stroked her wounded ego by offering her an alternate plan for the evening.

"If you'd let me buy you a drink in the lounge, I'd do my very best to replace that sad expression on your pretty face with a smile," he told her.

Where was she?

Travis was going out of his mind with worry. A couple of hours after the sun went down and Lauren still hadn't returned from town, he set aside his reservations about being the little boy who called wolf and contacted every single person he knew who might have any inkling of her whereabouts, effectively distributing his anxiety even among Lauren's friends and family.

"She left here hours ago," her mother informed him.

Travis regretted worrying her. Glad that she didn't chastise him for not treating her daughter right, he asked her if she knew of any reason that Lauren might be upset.

There was a long pause on the other end of the phone before Barbara responded. "I only know that she loves you madly—and she's afraid that you don't feel the same way about her."

That soft-spoken reprimand hit Travis with all the subtlety of a baseball bat. The memory of his silent response to Lauren's sweet, sweet admission of love stabbed through him, and he forgot about salvaging the tenuous good impression he'd made upon her family.

"I care very deeply about your daughter," he said.

"Then you might think about letting her know that— before you lose her altogether."

It was good advice. Travis just hoped it wasn't too late to follow it. If he had been unsure of his feelings for Lauren before, by the time he hung up the phone, there was absolutely no doubt left in his mind that he had fallen hopelessly in love with her. Why else would he become so physically sick with worry wondering where she was?

Travis imagined the worst. The possibilities were endlessly gruesome. He envisioned her bleeding to death by the side of road, wandering around the countryside in a state of amnesia, abducted and raped by some lunatic. The spike in his blood pressure was at a dangerous level. Exhausting the more grisly scenarios, he considered another possibility.

Maybe she was just playing mind games with him. Maybe she was more like Jaclyn than he wanted to think. Maybe she was down at The Alibi looking for a less emotionally constipated man who didn't swallow his tongue whenever she expressed her feelings for him.

At a loss what to do, Travis climbed into his pickup in a self-induced panic and set out to find her. He tried the bars first. There was no sign of her there. Nor on any of the side streets in Pinedale. His friend Larry at the police station informed him that they could not put out an all-points bulletin for a single woman who had been missing for less than twenty-four hours.

"And I hate to tell you, but you don't have any legal rights over someone who isn't your wife."

Leaning over the counter, Travis took a combative stance. Jaclyn had tried provoking him into such a fit of fury on more than one occasion and had done little more than irritate him. This was different from such manipulative ploys. Travis had to believe that Lauren wouldn't play those kind of sick games.

Stepping back, Larry hastened to expound his official position.

"Listen, buddy, I'm sorry to see you in such a state, but this sounds more like a personal issue than a criminal one. I don't know how long the two of you have been together, but since when is Lauren required to report in to you?"

Travis backed off. Not because he wanted to. But because he had no other choice but to spend the night in jail if he didn't. The fact that Larry made him feel like some overprotective Neanderthal without a clue how to treat a lady didn't set well with him. Probably because he resembled the comparison more than he cared to admit.

"Sorry to take my frustrations out on you," Travis said. "But if I don't hear something from Lauren soon, I promise I'll be back in here demanding action."

Just a few short weeks ago Lauren would have been tempted to accept the stranger's offer to buy her a drink and strike up a conversation with a prospective bridegroom. Today she opted for a hot bath instead. No longer satisfied to be with just any man, she had her heart set on Travis. No one else would do.

Lauren filled the tub with hot water and eased herself in. Nothing in the world calmed her nerves like a good long soak. Placing a steaming washcloth over her face, she let the mystical properties of the bath dissolve the world beyond her skin. Much later when the water grew tepid and her skin turned the texture of prunes, she drained the liquid from the tub and felt the tension in her body melt away. By the time she stumbled to bed and said a little prayer that the path she was meant to take would be clearly laid out in front of her tomorrow, she was already half-asleep.

Twelve

Lauren squinted at the clock beside her bed. Her eyes widened in disbelief. It was almost past check-out time. She couldn't remember the last time she'd slept till noon. Awakening with a renewed sense of energy, she decided it was a whole lot easier to be a clear-thinker when Travis wasn't around to turn her brains to mush. Playing the part of the invisible woman for the past few years had certain advantages. While everyone had been busy ignoring her, Lauren learned how to think for herself and become her own person. A good night's sleep brought with it the realization that it didn't matter what anyone else thought. And that, no matter how well intended others might be, she shouldn't let anyone else define her dreams.

Quite simply Lauren wanted it all. To be married. To be a wife and a mother as well as a lover. She believed herself deserving of a tried and true happy ending complete with a preacher and a multitiered cake and a bouquet that she got to throw instead of catch for once.

As humble as her dream might be, she decided that it was worth holding out for.

Pride put a steel rod in her spine and prevented Lauren from accepting less than the real deal. She was tired of crying her eyes out over someone who didn't appreciate her, and she wasn't willing to settle for just marrying anyone for the sake of a ring and the approval of polite society, either. Nor did she want to force a man into marriage against his will. If she were pregnant with Travis's child after their last passionate encounter, she would rather die than use an innocent baby as a bargaining chip to get what she wanted from him.

"I'm an intelligent, attractive and independent woman," she told herself. "I don't need a man to make me whole. Certainly not one with a reputation of abandoning women as soon as he grows tired of them."

Of course, that didn't change the fact that she loved Travis.

She was willing to stake her future on the idea of the two of them being together for a lifetime. The question was whether he loved her and was willing to take a chance on marriage. If he wasn't smart enough to see what a terrific catch she was, he could go hang out at

The Alibi for the next decade or so and wait for someone better to come along.

Lauren understood that she could no more commandeer Travis's love than she could continue to resent her father for dying. The only solution that left her a modicum of dignity was to embrace herself as a wonderful, sensual creature entitled to a lifetime of self-love and approval. Time would tell whether Travis would come around.

If he didn't love her enough to marry her, she decided that she would simply have to love herself all the more.

Lauren rushed to make herself presentable before check-out time. Staring into the mirror, she looked deep into her own eyes and assured herself that everything was going to work out all right. Then she shut off the light and headed out to do a little shopping. There were a few things she wanted to buy before confronting Travis on his home turf. They included candles, chocolate, a bottle of wine and the most elegant negligee she could find.

It was dark by the time Lauren got back to the ranch. An ominous sense of foreboding settled over her as she shut off her vehicle and stepped into the obscurity of a night illuminated only by the canopy of stars overhead. She suddenly felt very small.

And all alone.

There was not a single light on in either the big house or the cabin. It was one thing to imitate Katherine Hepburn's sense of independence in the bright light of day but much harder to attempt it while fumbling for her keys in the darkness while thinking about confronting the man who made her feel as vulnerable as a kitten. She finally managed to open the front door and flip the light switch on. Everything was neat and orderly as she'd left it. The boogey man was nowhere to be seen.

And neither was Travis.

Lauren told herself that it was silly to be disappointed that he wasn't there waiting for her. That he wasn't the least bit worried about her. Not that she owed him any explanations about her whereabouts. She'd just hoped that absence might have made his heart grow fonder. All the way home, she fantasized about him waiting there for her, ready to present her with the ring he'd bought after having a change of heart.

Disappointment was a bitter, though not wholly unexpected, pill to swallow.

Unable to imagine where he could be at this time of night, Lauren assumed he simply had turned in early after a long day's work. The man did work hard—much harder in fact than she had ever supposed before getting to know him better. Travis Banks was far less of the playboy that she'd always imagined him to be and more of a regular working guy who didn't take his stewardship over the land lightly. More often than not, that meant long hours of toil in the elements and nights shortened by the necessary paperwork required to keep a ranch this size running smoothly.

Lauren couldn't help but worry that he might have been tossed from his horse and lay helpless at the bottom of some gulch, unconscious. Maybe he'd had an accident with some of the big equipment on the place. Maybe he was simply at the vet with a sick animal.

Alternate possibilities about where Travis might be were too painful to entertain. Just the thought of him with another woman was enough to make her physically ill.

Sanity demanded that she simply proceed with the ritual she'd devised to bolster her flagging courage, so she began setting the stage. She wasn't going to wait around any longer for the love that Travis was either unwilling or unable to give her. Lauren felt entitled to the romance that every woman craved, and didn't want to get it vicariously through movies, books or soap operas, either.

First, she placed a single long-stemmed rose in the center of the table and surrounded it with tall flickering tapers. Then she unpacked a fondue pot, broke a thick bar of imported dark chocolate into it and turned it to simmer. Wanting to believe that whatever was happening in her life was only a reflection of the limits she put on her own mind, Lauren decided it was time for her to trust the intelligence within.

It was time to woo herself and to indulge in the seduction of all of her senses.

Next she selected a CD of dreamy love songs and set a bottle of champagne into a silver bucket that she filled with ice. Then she rinsed and culled a pint of fresh strawberries the size of golf balls. These she placed in a pretty antique dish reserved for special occasions. Before taking a beautifully wrapped package into her bedroom, she took a moment to stir the chocolate in the fondue pot.

Sitting on the edge of the bed, she delighted in the crinkly sound of tissue paper as she lifted an outrageously expensive negligee out of the box. The floor-length gown was a whisper of gray satin trimmed in pink lace. Lauren paused to touch the cool, slick fabric to her cheek before slipping out of her regular clothes and transforming herself into a movie star. It was as if the negligee had been custom-made to mold to the curves of her body. Twirling around in front of a full-length mirror, she'd never felt more beautiful.

And regretted only that Travis wasn't there to see her in it.

She returned to the other room to take her place of honor at a candlelit table set for one. Taking a silver skewer in one hand, she stabbed a strawberry and swirled it into the rich, dark, melted chocolate. The aroma alone was enough to make her mouth water in anticipation. It took a certain amount of self-control to admire the artistry of her creation before sinking her teeth into it.

Ah…heaven!

Lauren washed down the aphrodisiac with champagne from a delicate crystal flute. The bubbles tickled her throat. Her second glass made her feel a little bit fuzzy. Lifting it in the air, she offered a toast as a way of kicking off the symbolic private ceremony designed to mark the beginning of her life as an enlightened creature capable of making herself happy—or at least being content in solitude of her own company.

"Here's to you, baby," Lauren said to herself.

After devouring as many chocolate-covered strawberries as her stomach could hold, she gave herself over to bedtime. She didn't bother blowing the candles out. She drew back her sheets and sprinkled them with the essence of violets. Sheathed in satin, she slid between those perfumed sheets, fluffed her pillow and promptly burst into tears.

Lauren wondered just how long she'd been undiagnosed as a schizophrenic.

Love was an ill-mannered beast capable of turning a once strong-willed woman into someone incapable of making up her mind about anything: whether to sleep with Travis or not, whether to live with him or without him, whether to cry or to laugh at the ridiculousness of her dilemma. Lauren couldn't understand why it was so difficult for him to say he loved her. Why she was good enough to sleep with but not to marry? Why, in spite of her best efforts to hold herself to a higher standard, she could not simply walk away with her head held high and her dignity intact?

The answer to those questions seemed to lie in the fact that the bed was too big without Travis in it and that she hadn't managed a single bite of food all night without thinking about him.

Without missing him desperately.

All her elaborate ritual had accomplished was to prove once and for all that love was more powerful than pride. What good was pretending when she couldn't even manage to fool herself? As a modern, enlightened woman, Lauren might not need a man to make her feel complete, but she needed Travis in order to *feel* anything at all.

In the dark of the night, in the middle her lonely bed, Lauren had an epiphany. Love didn't make demands based on what others might think or do out of a sense of obligation to the outdated dreams spawned in a young girl's heart and attached to the sentimentality of a previous era. It was wrong of her not to accept Travis as he was and where he was right now. Calling herself stupid and headstrong, she realized that Suzanne and her mother were both right.

Rather than bemoaning the fact that Travis wasn't ready for the kind of commitment she wanted, Lauren knew she should grab onto what he was offering with both hands and hang on for life. It was time for her to put aside unicorns and pixie dust and childish fairy tales. Time to grow up and act like a woman, not a little girl perpetually trying to please an absent father who would not have loved her any less without the unrealistic expectations she placed upon herself in his name.

Lauren hoped it wasn't too late and that Travis hadn't changed his mind. First thing in the morning she intended to march right over to his house and see if she couldn't set things right between them. Maybe if she arrived with her suitcase in hand, he wouldn't have the heart to turn her away.

* * *

When Travis pulled into the driveway well after midnight and saw Lauren's car parked in front of the cabin, he couldn't remember ever being so relieved.

Or upset.

Lauren had better have one hell of an explanation for taking off without letting him or anyone else know where she was going or what she was doing. Responsible, mature women simply didn't disappear without a word to anyone. Just thinking about her foolish behavior got him so riled up that he had half a mind to knock on her door right now, and give her a good tongue-lashing. Right after he gave her a good tongue-lashing…

Damn it, why couldn't he keep his mind off sex for more than ten minutes at a time when it came to anything having to do with Lauren? As tired as Travis was, he was surprised his body could respond like this. He felt like he'd aged more over the past forty-eight hours than in the last two years.

Didn't Lauren realize how worried he would be about her? How much he loved her?

How could she?

Guilt pierced his heart with a broken blade. Unless she was a mind reader, it would be impossible for her to know that crucial piece of information. He hadn't been able to tell her the other day when she so desperately needed to hear it. Travis himself hadn't admitted the depth of his feelings until she turned up missing and he'd gone completely out of his mind with worry. What a shame that she had to leave him just to get something so important through his thick skull.

He loved her!

By now everyone in town knew it, except Lauren herself. Travis Banks, self-proclaimed bachelor for life, was madly, passionately, head over heals, crazy in love with a woman who refused to put up with his halfhearted way of living. Oddly enough he loved her for it. He loved everything about her: her strengths and her foibles; her innocence and her lack of inhibition; her stubbornness and her pride; her strange sense of humor; her unpredictable and ever-changing mind.

Travis couldn't afford to waste another minute keeping such a wonderful revelation to himself. High on love and caffeine, he started down the path to her home determined to wake Lauren up, if necessary, to tell her exactly what was on his mind. What he had to say would probably be better articulated in the morning, but he couldn't wait that long.

He hadn't been able to sleep a wink or hold down much more than coffee—pots of the strongest stuff he could find—ever since realizing that Lauren was nowhere to be found. The combination of sleep deprivation and excessive amounts of caffeine had made him less than pleasant to be around. His friends down at the police station and the sheriff's office could testify to that fact—and probably would in court if any of them decided to press charges. Having just returned from making a scene down there in his attempt to get someone to take Lauren's disappearance seriously, he hadn't endeared himself with the local authorities.

In fact, after making a complete ass of himself, he

wasn't looking forward to telling Larry that he'd been right all along. Travis had simply overreacted, Lauren was just fine, and everything was back to normal.

Or was it?

The closer Travis got to Lauren's front door, the more bewildered he became. Candles cast a soft glow through the picture window illuminating a cozy, suggestive scene. An open bottle of champagne and the remnants of a scrumptious romantic dinner were left out on the table. And a filmy robe was draped over the back of one chair....

Thunder rumbled in the distance. Suddenly Travis was glad he hadn't decided to phone the police. If he couldn't get himself under control in the next few minutes, they might just have to arrest him for murder.

Thirteen

Not jealous by nature, Travis was overwhelmed by the intensity of emotion that made his blood boil. He'd heard of people seeing red before, but until now had never experienced the phenomenon himself. Rage clouded his vision and left him reeling on the porch. He reached for the railing to steady himself and nearly tore it off its foundation. Seeing only one vehicle parked out front he'd jumped to the conclusion that Lauren had picked up someone on her road trip and brought him back here—to flaunt in his face.

He raised his hand in a fist but couldn't bring himself to knock on the front door.

The thought of finding Lauren in bed with someone else brought with it a hot smack of anger that nearly doubled him over. No wonder some men turned a blind eye to their wives' infidelities. Denial had to be easier than facing such unbearable agony.

What an idiot he was, naively believing Lauren to be beyond the petty mind games that other women played. Like a blithering fool, he'd put her on a golden pedestal. And spent the past couple of days feeling guilty about compromising such a fine woman by asking her to move in with him and treating her as though she was nothing more than a college roommate rather than a precious object worthy of all his love.

The thought that he'd been on his way over here to propose to her turned his stomach.

The truth of the matter was that Lauren was no better than Jaclyn, the master manipulator who'd taught him better than to place his trust in any woman. Her behavior was contemptible. Like his ex-wife, Lauren was obviously out to prove that she could do exactly what she wanted with her life without regard to his feelings. And while it was true that he and Lauren weren't married, and therefore, as his friend Larry so drolly pointed out as two of his fellow officers did their best to restrain Travis, had no jurisdiction over what she did with her life. But that didn't mean they had no moral obligation to each other. He thought they shared something special. A one of a kind love that poets immortalized and movies did their best to imitate.

If Lauren was trying to make him jealous, she'd succeeded as no other woman had before. But it would be her undoing rather than her crowning joy. He'd damned well see to that when she came crawling back and asking for his forgiveness.

Travis wondered if she fully understood just how dangerous a game it was that she was playing. Men had gone to prison for what he was contemplating.

The smartest thing he could do would simply be to march back home the same way he'd come and never once let on how much Lauren's little ploy got to him. Pride and a gallon of whiskey were calling his name.

But anger's pull was stronger.

Travis wondered what it said about him that he still loved Lauren in spite of her betrayal. He despised himself and was suddenly glad that he hadn't openly expressed the depth of his feelings for her since that was the only thing sparing him from absolute and total humiliation.

He tried the front door and was surprised to find it unlocked. Making no attempt to be sneaky, he threw it open and stomped inside. He then made a beeline directly to the bedroom without pausing to notice that only a single champagne flute stood on the table. It took a little while for his eyes to adjust to the fading candlelight. He tripped over a package on the floor, causing him to announce his presence with an oath.

"Who's there?" Lauren called out.

Heart pounding, she sat up in bed and reached for the lamp beside her bed. In a state of confusion, she knocked it over without managing to turn it on. A dark, hulking figure stood in the doorway of her bedroom breathing heavily. Grabbing a decorative conch shell from the bed stand, she armed herself for battle. She wasn't sure whether it would be wiser to throw the object or wait until the intruder attacked to hit him over the head with it.

"Who the hell do you think it is?"

Recognizing the sound of that deep, angry voice, Lauren dropped her weapon with a thud. She felt hot, cold and trembly all over as adrenaline seeped from her body. Her fingers tingled, her head ached and tears sprang to her eyes.

"Travis, you scared me to death!"

Mumbling something incoherent in response, he switched on the overhead light and squinted at her with an expression of utter contempt on his face. A veritable stranger with eyes capable of burning holes right through her replaced the sweet and gentle lover she had left less than two short days ago. His hands were curled into fists, and he looked ready to burst out of his shirt any minute.

Lauren had never seen him in such a state. A throbbing vein in his temple worried her. Her mother might label this a conniption fit, but Lauren worried he was on the verge of a stroke.

"What's wrong?" she asked, throwing back her covers.

A twinge of guilt told her that she should have let him know where she was going the other day, but at the time Lauren hadn't exactly known herself. Besides nothing she had or hadn't done warranted this kind of bizarre behavior. Did she really want to be with someone who looked like he wanted to murder her?

Pressing her back against the headboard, Lauren asked, "Have you been drinking?"

Travis looked her up and down in an insolent gesture. Aware of her nipples showing through a nightgown purposely designed to emphasize the swell of her breasts, Lauren instinctively reached for her sheet, which she proceeded to pull up to her chin.

"Where is he?" Travis demanded to know.

He had nothing against Lauren sleeping in the nude with him, but it rankled that she would buy such sexy lingerie for another man. A man he intended to tear limb from limb while she watched.

She looked around in confusion.

"Who?"

Not to be so easily duped by a pair of big, innocent-looking eyes or a pair of shapely breasts, Travis ripped the bathroom door open. And found the tiny room unoccupied. He drew the shower curtain back and found no sign of intrusion.

Undeterred, he stamped over to Lauren's closet and almost pulled the door off its hinges. Empty hangers clattered against the back wall, and clothes shifted with the impact of the breeze he created. But nobody darted between the feet Travis planted directly in front of the door like an angry giant. A giant who felt himself shrinking to the size of a mouse with the dawning realization that he had made one whopper of a mistake.

"Who are you looking for?"

Travis checked to see that the window was closed and the curtains weren't stirring from a hastily planned retreat. Nothing. Clearly there was nobody else here but the two of them. His first reaction at being so obviously mistaken was one of complete and utter relief. Sinking onto the foot of Lauren's bed, he bowed his head as fury turned to shame.

Had God ever put a bigger fool on the planet?

Travis couldn't fathom what kind of power this woman wielded to turn him into such a mindless brute. He couldn't believe that he'd actually leaped to such an awful conclusion without giving Lauren the benefit of the doubt. He hoped that he hadn't scared her so badly that she never wanted to see him again.

The sight of her shocked face made him feel like a monster. He might throttle her imaginary lover within an inch of his life, but surely Lauren knew that he could never, ever hurt her.

How could he possibly rationalize such a display of jealous stupidity? Lack of food and sleep hardly sufficed as a reasonable explanation. Utterly embarrassed by his actions, Travis invented several elaborate lies on the spot.

An escaped convict was on the loose in the vicinity. A rabid mountain lion was sighted in the area. The FBI had issued an all-points bulletin for a group of terrorists headed this way. A one-armed man...

Ultimately he settled on a cryptic version of the truth.

"It appears that I'm looking for the fellow who made a full-blown idiot come to his senses."

Lauren looked at him as if he was crazy.

"What are you talking about?"

As much as Travis wanted to put her mind at ease, he didn't exactly want to insult her with actual facts, either. He doubted she'd be flattered by his assumption she had brought another man into their bed. Hoping to deflect attention away from his bad behavior, he employed a sweeter tone of voice as he began slowly inching his way up the bed toward her. The gleam in his eye made her squirm.

"Suffice it to say I misplaced my sanity for a minute, and I thought you, my little runaway, might be hiding it. Do you think it might be under the sheets somewhere?"

"Maybe you should check under the bed," she suggested dryly.

If he could manage to kiss her within the next minute, Travis thought he might still have a chance to skirt over the reason behind his temporary insanity.

"Did I mention how relieved I am that you're home?" he asked, with a touch of censure in his voice.

"I'm sorry. Really I am. I should have called."

Travis's whole world lit up. A heart that had shriveled in his chest at the idea of her cheating on him swelled in sudden exultation and banged against his ribs. Maybe if he could make her sorry enough about worrying him half to death, she would overlook his caveman routine and even let him peek beneath that pretty nightie. She could pose for a centerfold wearing that mouthwatering little thing.

Although Travis would much prefer she model it for him alone.

"I got home quite a while ago. Where have you been?"

The question stopped Travis in the middle of his trek up the length of the bed. Indignation pushed its way to the forefront of his jumbled emotions.

"Do you really have the audacity to ask me where *I've* been?"

Lauren's voice was as tiny as a mouse's. "I didn't mean for you to worry."

"And are you sure that wasn't the idea?" Travis demanded. "To worry me out of my mind and bring me to my knees?"

Lauren blushed.

"Okay, I'll admit it. In the back of my mind I did hope you'd miss me while I was away. But mostly, I just needed to do some soul searching, and since I don't seem to be able to think very clearly when you're around distracting me with your kisses, I took some time to sort things out by myself."

Speaking of distractions, Lauren reached over to fondle him.

Suddenly Travis couldn't think very well, either. At least not with the head on his shoulders.

"Besides I didn't think I needed your permission to leave the premises," she said, giving a gentle squeeze.

Travis's voice grew raspy. "And did you come to any conclusions while you were gone?"

"I did. But maybe we shouldn't discuss this in bed," Lauren suggested. The mysterious smile that crept across her face was reminiscent of Mona Lisa's.

As little as he liked the sound of that, Travis *was* having trouble concentrating at the moment. With great effort he removed her hand from where it rested and pulled himself up to sit beside her. The brass headboard at his back pressed against a wall of burnished logs.

"If you promise to keep your hands to yourself, I'll promise to stay on my side of the bed until we resolve our differences," he said.

Primly, Lauren folded her hands on the outside of the bedding. "It's a deal."

A light rain began pattering against the tin roof, playing the refrain of a love song as eternal as the dark mountain silhouetted in the moonlight outside. After long days of drought and doubt, a sudden shower arrived to wash away the last traces of human pride. Lauren looked deeply into Travis's eyes.

"You'll be glad to know that while I was gone I came to terms with life as a single woman. I decided that it was wrong to try and pressure you into doing anything that makes you uncomfortable just to make me happy. You should do what makes *you* happy."

The scent of Lauren's perfume made Travis happy. The sparkle in her eyes. The lilt of her laugh. The warmth of her touch. And the way she made him feel when he was around her.

Just as soon as she finished being so very selfless, he intended to tell her as much. *She* made him happy.

Wearing a look of complete earnestness, Lauren continued. "It would be wrong of me to hold you to some outdated social mores that don't necessarily fit anymore. I have no right to ask you to be anything but who you are. I do love you, Travis Banks, but you're probably right about us needing more time to get to know one another."

Travis couldn't have looked more startled. Was Lauren having second thoughts about wanting to get married? As mercurial as her moods were, he just might end up losing her yet if he didn't pin her down soon.

"What exactly are you trying to say, Lauren?"

"That I'd like to move in with you—if you haven't changed your mind about it, that is."

A week ago, Travis might have felt as though he'd won by getting such a huge concession. Today, Lauren's declaration only deepened his desire to commit to something more formal and binding. Something that would last forever.

"I have," he stated emphatically. "I most definitely have changed my mind."

Lauren dropped her head and stared at the hands folded in her lap. To keep them from shaking, she clenched them so tightly together that they turned a ghastly shade of white. She bit her lip—hard—and tasted blood. Her mother and Suzanne had both warned her this might happen. She'd had her chance at happiness and screwed it up royally.

And she had no one to blame but herself.

Lauren couldn't fault Travis for changing his mind after the childish stunt she'd pulled. Hot, stinging tears came to her eyes. She forced them back. Knowing that making a scene wouldn't do anything but make matters worse, she somehow managed to give him a quavery smile.

"I understand," she said, willing her voice not to crack. "How soon do you want me to move out?"

"Immediately."

His blunt response hit her like a volley of machine gun fire. Numbly, she attempted to salvage the remaining shreds of her dignity. She threw back the comforter and tried to get out of bed without somehow falling down. Travis grabbed her by the arm and pulled her back beside him.

"I don't think you do understand," he said.

"Yes, I do," she croaked, resenting him for making this so much harder than it had to be. Couldn't he just let her go and allow her the dignity of crying her heart out in private?

"I want to marry you, Lauren. I want to make you my wife."

Thinking that she had misheard him, Lauren clarified her position one more time.

"I already told you. You don't have to marry me. I'm not pregnant if that's what you're worried about, and even if I were, I'd be okay. Actually I really *am* okay. With or without a ring."

Travis's smile reached his eyes and gave Lauren reason for hope.

"I know you are, but I'm not okay with any kind of half-baked commitment from you. I think it's safe to say that I want a whole lot more from you than just conjugal rights. And for what it's worth, I'm disappointed that you're not pregnant. Nothing in this world could make me any happier than to have a baby with you. Ever since you left I've been thinking about what my life was like before you waltzed into it. I assure you it's a very sad and lonely existence.

"And one more thing," he added gazing deep into her eyes. "Whether you intended for me to worry about you or not isn't the question. Believe me, sweetheart, I worried."

He put a finger to her lips before she could apologize again. Though she couldn't keep from kissing it, she refrained from doing what she really wanted—gobbling him up whole starting with that one delectable fingertip.

"By the way," he continued, "I hope you called your mother to let her know you're safe. A lot of people besides me have been worried sick about you."

Lauren had the good sense to look embarrassed. She hadn't thought anyone would miss her for so short a time and supposed she could point a finger at Travis for getting everyone stirred up.

"I didn't realize—" she began.

"Me, either. That's the whole point. I didn't realize how important you are to me. How much I need you. How much I miss you when you're not around. How I can't function without you. When I thought you had another man in here, I completely lost it."

Unable to get past the words "another man" Lauren scrunched her face in perplexity.

"You thought what?"

"Oh, come on," Travis said in his own defense. "What was I supposed to think? Champagne, candles, mood music, sexy lingerie scattered on the furniture…"

His eyes turned dark and dangerous as an insidious possibility occurred to him.

"I hope you didn't stage that elaborate scene just to make me jealous."

Lauren's laughter put that worry to rest. She brushed her fingertips against his five o'clock stubble and said, "Didn't you once tell me you didn't have a jealous bone in your body?"

Rumor had it that many women had tried and failed miserably when playing that particular card with this hardheaded man.

"I didn't," he said, "before I met you."

A crooked smile played with the edges of Lauren's mouth. "So I take it you weren't just looking for the boogey man in my closet?"

"More like some smarmy con man you met on your trip."

Instantly the stranger who'd offered to buy her a drink popped into Lauren's mind, but she decided to keep that bit of information to herself. A little jealousy went a long way, and she didn't want Travis jumping in the truck to hunt the poor man down. Especially considering the fact that absolutely nothing had happened between them.

"So tell me about this little party you threw," Travis demanded. "And why, may I ask, wasn't I invited?"

Lauren searched for the right words with little success.

"It wasn't a party exactly. It was more…of a ritual… intended to help me … get over you."

Travis cocked an eyebrow at her quizzically. "I hope

it didn't involve a voodoo doll and an assortment of ac-upuncture needles."

Lauren looked shocked by the very idea. "Actually it was more along the lines of being good to myself and hoping love would naturally follow."

Travis slid off the bed to kneel before her.

"Then I guess it worked."

The moment Lauren had waited for all her life couldn't have seemed any more surreal. Touched by the raw emotion that brought this big man to his knees, she touched his temple with trembling hand. He took it in-to his own and kissed it in the center of her palm. One by one he claimed her fingers. Ripples of heat coursed up her arm. Her heart was beating so loudly that she was afraid she wouldn't be able to make herself heard over the thrumming in her own ears. She searched the depths of Travis's beloved gray eyes and saw his soul reflect-ed there.

"Will you make me the happiest man alive?" he asked.

There was only one other thing that would make this moment perfect.

Was it too much to ask that every single piece of the fairy tale fall into place? Would her insistence on forc-ing three little words from his mouth be her ruination? Lauren didn't want him to marry her just to control his newfound sense of jealousy. As risky as it was, she had to take the chance. Before she could say yes, she real-ized there was something she had to know.

"You haven't told me you love me," she pointed out in a whisper that trembled like a leaf.

"Sweetheart," Travis drawled, dissolving her misgivings with the endearment. "Love isn't a word that comes easy to me, but if you'll marry me, I'll work on making it a part of my daily vocabulary. I love you, Lauren. With all of my heart and all of my soul. I will until there's no breath left in me to breathe. If you will do me the honor of becoming my wife, I will cherish you, love you and hold you so tight you never have to question my feelings for you again."

Those sweet words echoed in the core of her being and filled an aching void. She answered the way that her heart dictated.

Taking his face in both her hands, Lauren smothered Travis with kisses before pulling him off his knees and into her bed. She spoke his name tenderly and drew him into her arms, welcoming him home the best way she knew how.

Tomorrow they would begin moving her things into the big house. Tomorrow they would begin making plans for their wedding, their marriage and their future family.

Tonight they would share a bed in the humble cabin that Travis's grandparents had christened with their love oh so long ago. They were both ravenous for the gourmet feast that awaited them, and it didn't have anything to do with the chocolate-covered strawberries waiting for them in the kitchen.

Epilogue

A hush fell over the crowd as a bouquet of pink roses, miniature white carnations and baby's breath tumbled end over end through the air above their collective heads. Some of the guests hardly recognized the woman who tossed it. Sheathed in an off-the-shoulder gown of antique ivory, she was the most enchanting creature they'd ever seen.

Mrs. Travis Banks was a definite turn-around from the plain English teacher they all knew. It was almost as if Lauren Hewett stepped out from under an invisibility cloak to reveal herself on this most auspicious day, the day the most unlikely candidate in town married Pinedale's most eligible bachelor.

Many were still reeling from the swiftness of the

deed. After all, it had only been a couple of short months ago that they had attended Barbara Aberdeen's wedding and felt a jolt of pity for her spinster daughter. Who would have guessed that she was capable of transforming herself from an ugly duckling to such a lovely swan right under their noses?

With tiny flowers and seed pearls sprinkled in her hair, Lauren was a picture-perfect bride. The flush in her cheeks was all her own as was the dazzling smile she gave her guests—and the tender glances saved for her husband alone. Never had they seen a more vibrant, beautiful bride. Nor such a handsome, happy groom. Travis surprised everyone by personally writing the vows he spoke aloud at the altar with never a quaver in his voice. The words he spoke were so sincere and moving that many in attendance were forced to bring out hankies and tissues.

Lauren's stepfather, Henry Aberdeen, walked her up the aisle, but a place of honor had also been reserved for a picture of Eugene Hewett. Smiling behind a gilded frame, he gave his blessing to his only daughter—the apple of his eye—and seemed to say that he would always be with her in spirit. Lauren told her mother that he had come to her in a dream and given the marriage his blessing.

When the time came for her to toss the bridal bouquet, several people remarked on the fact that the bride herself caught it at the last wedding they'd attended, thus lending even more credibility to the old wives' tale that helped keep that particular tradition alive. It did seem that more single women than usual crowded together at the foot of the winding stairway for a chance to be the next in line. Lauren turned her back like she was supposed to do to spare some poor woman the embarrassment she herself had endured by being singled out in advance at her mother's wedding.

But that didn't necessarily mean that Lauren didn't want a say in the outcome.

"Get ready," she warned with a giggle.

A second later she tossed the bouquet high in the air and far over the assembled mass of hopeful females. Her unknowing target was a shy wallflower who had barely moved from the spot where she'd been rooted for the better part of an hour. The poor thing couldn't have looked any more surprised when the bouquet fell into her hands and a cheer went up around her than had a fairy godmother suddenly appeared.

From her position at the top of the stairs, Lauren covertly gave the recipient a knowing wink.

* * * * *

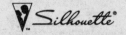

Silhouette

Desire

**Coming in June 2005
from Silhouette Desire**

Emilie Rose's

SCANDALOUS
PASSION

(Silhouette Desire #1660)

Phoebe Drew feared intimate photos
of her and her first love, Carter Jones,
would jeopardize her grandfather's
political career. So she went to Carter
for help finding them. But digging up
the past also uncovered long-hidden
passion, leaving Phoebe to wonder if
falling for Carter again would prove
to be her most scandalous decision.

*Available at your
favorite retail outlet.*

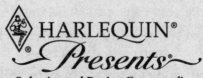

Silhouette Desire

COMING NEXT MONTH

#1657 ESTATE AFFAIR—Sara Orwig
Dynasties: The Ashtons
Eli Ashton couldn't resist one night of passion with Lara Hunter, the maid at Ashton Estates. Horrified that she had fallen into bed with such a powerful man, Lara fled the scene, leaving Eli wanting more. Could he convince Lara that their estate affair was the stuff fairy tales were made of?

#1658 WHATEVER REILLY WANTS…—Maureen Child
Three-Way Wager
All Connor Reilly had to do to win his no-sex-for-ninety-days bet was spend time with the one woman who wouldn't tempt him. Yet Emma Jacobsen had other plans, plans that involved a *very* short skirt and a change in attitude. Emma's transformation had Connor forgetting about his wager—but was what they had strong enough to last longer than ninety days?

#1659 SECRETS OF PATERNITY—Susan Crosby
Behind Closed Doors
Caryn Brenley and P.I. James Paladin had a son without ever meeting face-to-face *or* skin-to-skin. When Caryn learned James was her child's sperm donor, she reluctantly agreed to let father and son meet. James jumped at the opportunity, but pretty soon he wanted to get close to Caryn—the natural way.

#1660 SCANDALOUS PASSION—Emilie Rose
Phoebe Drew feared intimate photos of her and her first love, Carter Jones, would jeopardize her grandfather's political career. So she went to Carter for help in finding them. But digging up the past also uncovered long-hidden passion, leaving Phoebe to wonder if falling for Carter again would prove to be her most scandalous decision.

#1661 THE SULTAN'S BED—Laura Wright
Sultan Zayad Al-Nayhal came to California to find his sister, but instead ended up spending time with her roommate, Mariah Kennedy. Mariah trusted no man—especially tall, dark and gorgeous ones. True, Zayad possessed all of these qualities, but he was ready to plead a personal case that even this savvy lawyer couldn't resist.

#1662 BLAME IT ON THE BLACKOUT—Heidi Betts
When a blackout brought their elevator to a screeching halt, personal assistant Lucy Grainger and her sinfully handsome boss, Peter Reynolds, gave in to unbridled passion. When the lights kicked back in, so did denial of their mutual attraction. Yet Peter found that his dreams of corporate success were suddenly being fogged by dreams of Lucy….

SDCNM0505